Riley Mae
and the
Rock Shocker Trek

Other books in the growing Faithgirlz!™ library

Bibles

The Faithgirlz! Bible

NIV Faithgirlz! Backpack Bible

Faithgirlz! Bible Studies

Secret Power of Love

Secret Power of Joy

Secret Power of Goodness

Secret Power of Grace

Fiction

From Sadie's Sketchbook

Shades of Truth (Book One)

Flickering Hope (Book Two)

Waves of Light (Book Three)

Brilliant Hues (Book Four)

Sophie's World Series

Meet Sophie (Book One)

Sophie Steps Up (Book Two)

Sophie and Friends (Book Three)

Sophie's Friendship Fiasco (Book Four)

Sophie Flakes Out (Book Five)

Sophie's Drama (Book Six)

The Lucy Series

Lucy Doesn't Wear Pink (Book One)
Lucy Out of Bounds (Book Two)
Lucy's Perfect Summer (Book Three)
Lucy Finds Her Way (Book Four)

The Girls of Harbor View

Girl Power (Book One)
Take Charge (Book Two)
Raising Faith (Book Three)
Secret Admirer (Book Four)

Boarding School Mysteries

Vanished (Book One)
Betrayed (Book Two)
Burned (Book Three)
Poisoned (Book Four)

Nonfiction

Faithgirlz Handbook
Faithgirlz Journal
Food, Faith, and Fun! Faithgirlz Cookbook
Real Girls of the Bible
My Beautiful Daughter
You! A Christian Girl's Guide to Growing Up
Girl Politics
Everybody Tells Me to Be Myself, but I Don't Know Who I Am

Devotions for Girls Series

No Boys Allowed

What's a Girl to Do?

Girlz Rock

Chick Chat

Shine On, Girl!

Check out www.faithgirlz.com

The Good News Shoes

Riley Mae
and the
Rock Shocker Trek

BOOK ONE

Jill Osborne

ZONDERKIDZ

Riley Mae and the Rock Shocker Trek

Copyright © 2013 by Jill Osborne

This title is also available as a Zondervan ebook.
Visit www.zondervan.com/ebooks

Requests for information should be addressed to:
Zonderkidz, 3900 *Sparks Drive, Grand Rapids, Michigan* 49546

978-0-310-74294-4

Editor: Kim Childress
Art direction: Deborah Washington
Cover design and interior decoration: Jennifer Zivoin
Interior design: Ben Fetterley and Greg Johnson
Interior composition: Greg Johnson/Textbook Perfect

Printed in the United States of America

13 14 15 16 17 18 19 20 /DCI/ 20 19 18 17 16 15 14 13 12 11 10 9 8 7 6 5 4 3 2 1

To my daughter Jen,
and her daughters, Riley and Reagan.
No matter where life takes you,
in whatever shoes you are wearing,
always remember how much I love you!

"For shoes, put on the peace that
comes from the Good News
so that you will be fully prepared."

EPHESIANS 6:15 NLT

Chapter 1

My name is Riley Mae Hart, and I have the best shoe collection of anyone you know. Not the dressy ones that pinch your toes. I'm talking about the shoes you can *do* stuff in—like hike, run, jump, and play sports. I have at least a hundred pairs. And they didn't cost me anything! Well, that's not exactly true. I *did* pay in sweat, scrapes, lots of tears, and a broken bone or two. I know—that sounds bad. But it's really not, I promise. In fact, looking back, I wouldn't change a thing.

Let me explain.

It all started in second grade when Joey Larson told me that I couldn't play baseball with the boys on our street.

"Girls can't hit, *or* catch, *or* run, *or* slide. And they cry!"

I had news for Joey. I could hit, catch, run, and slide circles around him. And *if* those boys would have given me a chance to prove it, Joey would have been the one crying. But they never let me play.

Fine. So what if I didn't play sports in the neighbor-hood. Instead I signed up for sports leagues—where they *have* to let you play. And then, when they find out how good you are, they *beg* you to play. I've been begged to play on lots of teams since then, and Joey, well, he gave up sports a few years ago and now he just plays boring video games all day long.

That brings me to seventh grade and the shoe contract. My dad owns his own advertising business, and a new shoe company named Swiftriver hired him to help market a collection of athletic shoes for girls. On the last day of my summer vacation, Dad asked me to come down to his office and try some of them out. When I showed up, these guys in suits were there. They watched me try on about eight pairs of shoes, and they wrote down everything I said about them. Of course, I said a lot of good things, 'cause they were really awesome shoes. Cute, too.

Finally, this one guy says, "Bart [that's my dad's name], your daughter is fabulous. Why don't we use her as our spokesgirl for the shoe line?" Then he says to me, "What's your name again, sweetie?"

I hate being called sweetie, but I tried to be polite.

"Riley—Riley Mae. The Mae comes from my dad's mom. I like to use both names because then when people hear my name they'll know I'm a girl."

The head suit guy scratched his head. "Hmmmm.

The *Riley Mae Sport Collection … so they'll know you're a girl!* That's catchy. I say we do it, Bart."

My dad looked up from the floor where he was reorganizing all the shoes I had flung around the office.

"Ummm … wow, I dunno … I'll have to talk with Lynda [that's my mom], and I'm not sure Riley really has the time to—"

"Dad—check out these hikers! They're sparkly!" I spun around in his office chair with my feet in the air. I guess that wasn't really the proper thing to do with those suit guys there, but the shoes got me all excited.

Another guy spoke up. "We could do all the photo shoots on weekends and during her school breaks. Tell Lynda that we'll pay for you and her to come along on any of the planned trips. What could be better than going on some free vacations?"

The spinning made me dizzy, so I stopped. I looked at my dad, and he looked as white as a ghost. For a minute I figured I had embarrassed him with all the spinning around. I found out later that he was just freaked out about the spokesgirl thing. It didn't sound like such a big thing to me, but I didn't realize what a spokesgirl was yet.

Chapter 2

I found out later that night that being a spokesgirl for a shoe company was a big enough deal to cause a family meeting—you know, where you all sit around the dining room table and look serious.

"I don't know, Bart. Having Riley's picture on advertisements makes me nervous." My mom's the chief of police of Clovis (that's in California near Fresno), so she tends to be suspicious of lots of stuff.

"I agree. They'd probably want her to do commercials too."

"Heavens, I don't want to get into all that."

I hate when parents talk about you like you aren't there. "Ummm … Mom? Dad? Can I say something?"

"I think it will be okay, Lynda. Either you or I will be there for every shoot."

"And what about Riley's school work?"

"They said she could do everything on weekends and during her school breaks."

I was beginning to think I wasn't needed at this meeting. I looked down under the table at my new pair of pink running shoes that the guys at the office let me have. I also spied a bug crawling across the floor. (I let the lucky thing get away. No sense squashing him and messing up the shoes.)

"Mom, can I go call TJ and tell her about the shoes?" (That's my best friend, Taylor Joy—another girl with a first name that makes you wonder.)

"Riley, we're in a meeting here."

"But you and Dad aren't letting me talk."

Dad peeked at me over the top of his reading glasses. "I'm sorry, honey. There are just some things you don't understand."

"I understand that I like sports and shoes. And I'd like to go on free vacations and be in commercials."

"Of course you would," Mom said. "But it's a lot of work, and you'll get tired of it after awhile. I know how you are."

I rolled my eyes. Maybe I'm like that a little, but I do stick with things that are really fun, like softball.

"We need some time to pray about this—see what God has in mind." Good reminder from Dad.

"So, if God says yes, can I do it?" I didn't know *how* we would know if God said yes, but I thought I'd ask anyway.

My parents both shrugged and looked at each other. That was a trick question—I admit it. They could only say yes to that one.

"Okay," Dad said. "Let's give it a month or so, and if God says yes, we'll do it."

The head suit guy from Swiftriver—I found out his name was Bob Hansen—came over three days later.

"Bart, I need an answer. We have photo shoots to schedule. Girls' softball season is practically here, and we've gotta get these Riley Maes on some feet."

They had already started putting my name on the shoes, and the reason I knew that was Mr. Hansen brought over five pairs of softball cleats for me to try on. They were amazing! They weren't just like the boys' shoes with girl-colored stripes—they had different designs in lots of different colors. I decided to wear the ones with the hot pink daisies over a yellow background.

"Can I go try these outside?" I was pretty sure Mom didn't want me sliding in the house.

She didn't answer. Instead she just said, "Bart, can we talk about this in the kitchen?"

Mr. Hansen told me I could go out.

The cleats worked great, and they were so pretty! I just wanted to run and run and never stop. My name was sewn in on the tongue of the shoe, and a daisy dotted the "i" in Riley—so cool! But the biggest surprise was when I slid into second base (I made up a little softball field in my backyard with bases and every- thing), and I saw the bottom of the shoes. There were my initials—RM—in big pink cursive letters.

That's when I knew that I *really* wanted to do this spokesgirl thing.

When I went back in the house, Mr. Hansen was handing out schedules.

"You've already got the year planned out?" Dad rubbed the back of his neck—that means he's stressed. Mom took down her Bible calendar from the refrigerator and started shaking her head. Mr. Hansen grinned from ear to ear. He has really white teeth.

"Relax, you two. Almost all the photo shoots are local. We're doing the first one right down the street at the baseball field. The boys' team is ready to go as soon as we are."

"A boys' team?" I asked. "But these shoes are for girls."

"Well, of course. But get this ..." Mr. Hansen moved into the center of the living room and started acting out the commercial idea. "We're going to have you show up in the middle of the boys' game, do some spectacular plays, and then at the end of the commercial, you slide into home plate. SAFE! The catcher will notice the shoes and scratch his head. Then when you take off your helmet, your ponytail will fall out, and the slogan will come up on the screen: 'The Riley Mae Sport Collection—so they'll know you're a girl.' Get it? You have as much skill as the boys, but you love being a girl so you wear Riley Mae shoes, which are—"

"Really girly!" I finished his sentence by plopping

down on the couch and lifting my feet with the flowery cleats up into the air.

Mom shook her head. "Bob, we haven't signed a contract yet."

"And we really need to pray about it a little longer." Dad rubbed his neck some more.

"I'll tell you what." Mr. Hansen smiled and pulled a stack of papers out of a briefcase. "Read this through and jot down any questions you have. Highlight anything you don't like. We'll change whatever you want us to change."

"What is that?" I jumped off the couch and ran over to look at the papers.

"It's your contract." Mr. Hansen handed it to my dad. "As soon as you're ready to sign, let me know. We'll get the baseball field reserved and then we'll film the commercial. It's gonna be great!"

Mr. Hansen is very enthusiastic. I bet he smiles in his sleep.

Chapter 3

We prayed a lot about that contract for the next couple of weeks. Each time I said "Amen," I got butterflies in my stomach, which reminded me of the Riley Mae softball cleats with the purple butterflies on them. They even have a name: "Butter Ups." I decided to wear those for the commercial, *if* my parents decided that God had said yes to the whole thing.

One night after dinner, Dad caught me modeling the Butter Ups in my full-length mirror.

"Hey, softball girl. Nice shoes."

I smiled. "Thanks, Dad. Hey—do you know what my favorite part is about the Riley Mae shoes?"

"Hmmm, let me see. It has to be the pink sparkly daisy that dots the "i" in your name on the tongue."

I gasped. "How did you know?"

"Because I've been watching you write your name like that for years. Who do you think suggested that logo?" He pointed his thumb to his chest.

I giggled and plopped down on my bed, where I had spread out a few different pairs of Riley Mae shoes. I held up the super-cute hiking boots called Rock Shockers.

"Wow, you really are an advertising genius! These shoes are amazing. Girls are going to buy them like crazy."

"Well, that's what we're all hoping for. But there's only one problem."

I sat up, startled. "What?"

"Swiftriver needs just the right spokesgirl, or it won't work. Someone who's enthusiastic, someone who's good at sports but can also be a good role-model …"

I jumped off the bed. "That's me!"

Dad crossed his arms and raised an eyebrow.

"Okay, I know I'm not perfect, but it could be me … right? If God says yes?"

I ran up to Dad and put my face near his. We sometimes play this spontaneous stare-down game to see who can go the longest without laughing. He lost immediately.

"Okay, Riley, here's the deal. Your mom and I think it would be a shame to have some other girl's name on those shoes. As we've been praying, we've realized that this will be a good opportunity for you to learn and to grow, and God's given us peace about letting you be the Swiftriver spokesgirl."

"Yes!" I jumped and pumped my fist in the air.

Dad laughed. "So we called Bob Hansen over to see about signing the contract. He's downstairs right now."

I flew by my dad, down the stairs, through the living room, and into the dining room, where a grinning Mr. Hansen sat, going over a stack of papers with my mom. Mom looked up, and then her eyes locked on my feet.

"Riley! Tell me you're not running around with cleats on in this house."

Mr. Hansen looked down at my Butter Ups. "Nice pick, Riley. Those are my faves." Then he winked at me. "I knew the minute we met that you were the right girl for Swiftriver."

The rest of the night was a blur. I was so excited that I had trouble concentrating as we read through the contract. Mom kept talking about how I was going to be busier than ever, and that I would have to keep my grades up. Dad explained that I would have to work with lots of professional people who would be telling me what to do. Mr. Hansen explained that I would be working a lot on weekends. I didn't care. I agreed to it all.

On his way out the door, Mr. Hansen handed me a cute sparkly-orange pen. It had a running shoe on it that said "RileyMae.com."

"I have a website? This is unbelievable! I'm going to check it out right now!"

"Well, it won't go live until after we air the commercial, but I expect we'll have tons of online sales. If we hurry, we can get this ball rolling by Thanksgiving so parents can buy the shoes for their girls for Christmas."

I couldn't think of *anything* any girl would want more.

Chapter 4

It seemed like forever, but Thanksgiving weekend finally arrived, and like Bob Hansen promised, so did the day of the commercial shoot. My whole family arrived early, since my parents had a few more questions for Bob. As we pulled up to the field, we saw that the boys' team was warming up, and the film crew was setting up their equipment.

Mom, who was wearing her full police uniform with all her weapons attached, pulled Mr. Hansen aside. "It says on page four of the contract that Riley will be in magazines. What magazines? I want to be able to say no if I don't approve of the magazine."

Mr. Hansen smiled and popped a mint into his mouth. "We totally understand. We're talking mostly sport mags, some teen stuff, and outdoor sport publications. We'll make sure you approve before we put the ad in."

"What about Brady? It doesn't say anything about him being able to come on the trips with us."

"Who's Brady?" Mr. Hansen shrugged.

That made me laugh.

Brady's my little brother. He's in third grade. He's really smart, but he's really weird. He doesn't have a lot of friends. I think it's because kids just don't *get* him, and neither do I. Here's what I'm talking about:

The day after my parents signed the shoe contract, Brady came into the living room where I was watching TV. He just stood there—staring at me, which was really annoying, so I turned off the TV and stared back.

"You don't look famous," he finally said.

"I'm not."

"Mom says she's afraid you're going to be."

"But I'm not."

"So what should I call you now?" This is a typical Brady question. He has this thing about what *he* likes to be called, and it's never "Brady." It's always some other character that he's pretending to be, or that he actually thinks he is. So we have to call him things like "Sailor Solomon," or "Supersonic Man," or "Prince Picklemeister."

See what I mean? Weird.

"Just call me Riley. Please."

He shook his head. "Riley isn't a famous name. I'd rather call you 'Princess Slide-a-Lot,' or 'Shoe Highness.'"

"Those are stupid names."

"How about 'The Fresno Bee-loved?'" (Our local newspaper is called the *Fresno Bee*.)

"NO."

"Okay, that's what I'll call you." Then he walked out.

I have to pray for a lot of patience with Brady. And when I can, I ignore him. Others do too, probably for the same reason.

But now Mom was making it impossible for Bob Hansen to ignore Brady. She asked him to sign a paper that said that Brady could be included in any and all Swiftriver activities.

"Sure," Mr. Hansen grinned and signed. "It's no trouble. No trouble at all."

Mr. Hansen obviously doesn't know Brady.

Right about then a couple of crazy people came running onto the field: a woman who was maybe in her thirties and was dressed super-nice, and a man who looked like a high school kid who just woke up and put on clothes that had been wadded up in a corner for a year or so.

"Flip, Fawn—meet our girl, Riley Mae, and her parents, Lynda and Bart." Mr. Hansen smiled through the introductions. "Oh … and, uh … Brady." He pointed to my brother, who was playing some silly boy game over on the bleachers. No one looked over there. Instead, Flip and Fawn just swarmed all over me like a bunch of bees.

"Oh, you are just perrrrrrfect for this job. Look at that hair!" Fawn (the woman) grabbed my head and pulled her fingers through my light-brown waves. Her right hand got caught.

"Owwww!" That was me, not her.

"That's okay, honey. I'll teach you how to brush your hair properly so that doesn't happen. How about a little green eye shadow to match those amazing eyes?"

"NO eye shadow. Riley doesn't wear makeup." Yep, that was Mom.

Fawn put her hand on her hip and sighed loudly. "I'm the makeup artist hired for this job, and I know what this girl needs."

My mom stood up on her toes so she was eye to eye with Fawn, who was wearing six-inch heels (which I thought was a funny choice since we were at a baseball field). "And I'm the mom and I say NO EYE SHADOW."

Fawn stepped back, and as she did, both of her heels sank into the dirt, so now Mom was looking down at her.

"Okay, then, how about a little blush and lip gloss?" Fawn stepped out of her shoes and pulled them out of the dirt to shake them off.

I don't know what Mom said then because Flip (the guy) pointed a camera at me and started asking me to do things.

"Smile! Frown! Laugh! Grimace!"

"Grimace? How's that different from a frown?" I was getting annoyed with that camera in my face.

"Try to look like you just drank bad milk."

Chapter 4

"Oh." I grabbed my stomach and pretended to throw up. Flip laughed and pretended like he was throwing up too. He went on and on with the gagging noises.

"Flip, this is a SERIOUS job! Do you THINK you could act like a professional for ONCE?" Fawn huffed and puffed her way over to me and smacked me in the face with a powder puff. (Well, I guess it was more like a gentle smack.) I choked on the dust and looked over at Flip, who was making fun of the way Fawn was smoothing her big blonde hairdo out of her eyes. Fawn turned and caught him—then she hit *him* in the face with the powder puff.

"Here's a clue, funny boy. Buy an iron." She tried to walk off in a hurry, but her heels kept sinking in to the dirt. I couldn't help cracking up.

"I just loooove working with her." Flip put his hand on his heart. Fawn turned and blew him a kiss.

Flip turned back to me. "Hey, Riley—you hungry?" He started pulling weird things out of his pockets. "I didn't have any breakfast. Luckily I always have some good stuff in here. If you see anything you want, help yourself."

He tossed a bunch of food items out on the ground: A piece of unwrapped beef jerky, a sandwich bag filled with some kind of cereal, a half-eaten granola bar, some random mints, and a fun-sized Snickers bar that looked like it had melted a few times and reformed into a triangle shape. He held the Snickers up and smiled.

"I bet you want this, don't you? All girls love chocolate."

"That's sick. How old is that candy bar?"

"Old? It's from Halloween. I think that's the last time I wore these pants."

"Well, at least we know it hasn't gone through the wash."

"Are you saying I don't wash my clothes? You're not gonna make fun of me like Fawn does, are ya?"

I looked over and noticed that Fawn and my mom were having a disagreement again. Their arms were flying all over the place. Nah, I didn't want to be like Fawn.

"I'm sorry. I didn't mean it." I tried to think of a way to make it up to him. "Okay, I'll take the Snickers." I ripped the wrapper off and popped it in my mouth. It wasn't so bad.

"You're a cool kid. I'm gonna like working with you." Flip took a bite of the jerky, made a face, and then spit it out.

"Whoa, I'm not sure what that was, but I can tell you one thing … it wasn't jerky!"

I grimaced. Flip took a picture of me.

"Perfect," he said.

My favorite part of the commercial shoot was when I slid into home plate. Flip suggested that they add some extra dirt to the area so that a big puff of it would fly up, and as the dirt settled, my shoes would dramatically come into view of all the confused boys. Too bad for Fawn, though. She got a little too close to home plate at the wrong time. Her nice white skirt isn't so white anymore.

Chapter 5

TJ's my best friend. We've known each other since kindergarten. So you can imagine how bugged I was that she was at her grandma's over Thanksgiving when all the shoe stuff was happening, and she wouldn't return my texts.

"My phone died and I forgot to bring my charger with me," was her excuse. "I can't believe you're in a commercial."

"And I can't believe I have a whole shoe collection named after me." I lifted up my foot and pointed to my name on a pair of green cross-trainers.

TJ shook her head. "I just don't get it. Why would they name shoes after *you*? It's not like you're famous. They usually name stuff after stars."

"Yeah, it's crazy how it all happened."

We walked together all the way to English class, and TJ didn't say another word, which meant something was up.

"TJ, are you okay?"

TJ took a brush out of her backpack and stroked it through her silky dark-brown hair, which perfectly matches her olive skin and brown eyes. I couldn't help thinking that she looks more like a shoe model than I do.

"Yeah, I'm fine. I was just thinking about softball season."

"That's all you ever think about. It's not even Christmas yet."

"I know, but did I tell you that Dad hired me a new pitching coach? I've been throwing every night. You wanna come hit some balls during Christmas break?"

"You know I do."

TJ's dad is our coach, and he's pretty serious about all the softball stuff. He had a batting cage built in the backyard of their house, and with the good weather in Fresno, we can pretty much practice all year long.

"I guess I have to keep getting better if I'm going to be a sports role model, right?"

That was meant to be kind of a joke, but TJ didn't laugh.

"Yeah … right."

I was pretty sure that my shoe contract was what was really bugging TJ, and I wanted to talk to her about it. But the bell rang for class, and TJ brought up softball again.

"Hey, put January 12th on your calendar. It's softball

signups, and as soon as we have our official roster, we can start practicing. Dad says with all the returning girls, we should have a championship season this year."

I smiled as I thought of the four-foot trophy with the number one on the top that could be ours in just a few short months.

"No prob. I'll be there."

Chapter 6

The thing I learned about contracts is that once you sign them, you have to do what they say or you get in trouble with ... I dunno ... someone important somewhere. Anyway, my contract with Swiftriver said that I had to appear at "the agreed-upon scheduled photo shoots." That was the schedule my mom had written on her Bible calendar. So you can imagine my surprise when instead of "Softball signups" on January 12th, the calendar said, "Swiftriver photo shoot—Fresno State University track."

"Can't we change it?" I pleaded with Mom while I laced up my bright orange Riley Mae running shoes. (Same ones that were on the pen Bob gave me.) "TJ's gonna kill me if I don't show up at signups."

"No, we can't change it. We talked about this, remember?" Mom had her hand on her hip.

I started running in place. The shoes felt really cushy.

"Talked about what?"

"About how you aren't going to be able to do all the things you normally do *and* be the Riley Mae shoe girl."

I stopped running and shrugged. "I remember you saying I'd be busy . . ."

Dad came in from the garage, tapping his watch. "Ready to go, girls? Where's Brady?"

"Riley doesn't want to do the shoot," Mom said. "She wants to go to softball signups instead."

"I didn't say I didn't want to do it. I just asked if we could change it."

Dad put his hand on my shoulder. "Of course we can't change it. And have you looked at your schedule for spring? You're not going to have time to play softball anyway."

Well—he might as well have hit me over the head with a softball bat!

Chapter 7

On the car ride over to the track, I looked over the Riley Mae photo shoot schedule. Why hadn't I paid attention to that before? I never thought I would have to give up softball. My dad was right, though—most of the Saturdays in March, April, and May were full, and that's when softball games were scheduled.

"TJ's gonna kill me. And then she'll never talk to me again."

"Well, if you're dead," Brady said, "then you won't care if she's not talking to you."

Dad looked back at me through the rearview mirror. "She'll understand, honey."

"No, she won't. I know my best friend." Correction—soon-to-be ex-best friend.

Just then a text came through on my phone.

Don't forget signups

1–3 today

C U soon

From TJ. I slammed the phone down on the seat. Not going to answer that. Maybe she would think my phone was dead.

"Dad, don't you think Swiftriver would *want* me to play softball, since I'm modeling softball cleats? Can't we just call Bob Hansen and ask—"

"Oh no, young lady." Mom turned to look at me and wagged her finger. "You SAID you were going to do this, so you're GONNA."

Dad pulled the car over to the side of the road.

"Brady, stay here. Ladies, join me outside."

Oh no, another family meeting.

Dad walked with me and Mom up and down the street for a minute, and he rubbed his stressed-out neck all the way. Then he bent down and looked me in the eyes. "Riley, when we signed the shoe contract, we agreed that for two years you would do photo shoots, magazine ads and commercials and appear at special events to help sell shoes." He pointed to my feet. "*Riley Mae* shoes. That's *you*. So *you* have to do this. We gave you all this information in advance, and you agreed to it all, or believe me, we wouldn't have decided to do this."

"I know, it's just that I didn't think I'd have to give up softball."

Mom took a deep breath. "Riley, we're sorry, but there's nothing we can do about it now. Maybe next year we can ask Bob to make some room in the schedule."

Just then, Brady jumped out of the car. He was messing with my phone.

"Put that down!"

"It's okay," he said. "TJ texted you again. I took care of it."

"What? That's MY phone. Gimme that! What did you write?"

I pulled up the sent messages. There it was. It was all over now.

Can't play softball.

Going to shoe shoot.

Fresno Bee-loved.

"BRADY!" I was going to say (okay, yell) more, but I noticed ten new text messages arriving in my inbox. They were all from TJ. They each had only one word:

U

R

SO

PLAYING

GIT

OVER

HERE

NOW

SHOE

GIRL

This was going to get ugly.

Chapter 8

The rest of the way to the track I was trying to figure out how to hurry up the photo shoot. It was for running shoes, so what if I just ran really fast? I decided I'd do everything they told me—even Fawn. It was ten o'clock, and I had until three o'clock to get to the softball field for signups. I still didn't know what to do about not having time to play softball, but if I just got there for signups maybe something would work out.

Thankfully the whole crew was all set up when we got there. Bob Hansen grinned as he opened the car door for me. I felt like some kind of famous person going to an awards show. Flip was eating Oreos—well, he was scraping the icing off with his teeth and putting the cookie parts in his shirt pocket. I guess for later. He must have eaten lots of icing by then because he was hyped-up. Good. Hyped-up would help with the hurry-up.

"Okay, Fawn, what are we doing with my hair today? Ponytail? Ribbons? Let's get this going." I had brushed all the tangles out before getting in the car. No need to be tortured by Fawn's fingers again.

"I was thinking we might cut your hair a little first. We're doing French braids, and your split ends are going to look like used paint brushes if we don't do sooooomething."

Ugh. French braids. Those would take a while.

It didn't end up taking as long as I thought because Fawn had a little accident with the scissors. Flip snuck up behind her and held an Oreo—just the cookie part— right in front of her face.

"Would you like a cookie?"

"DISGUSTING!" Fawn jumped back, which must have been hard in those tall leather boots of hers.

As she jumped, she lost her balance and used my hair as a sort of rope with one hand to hold herself up. The other hand—the one with the scissors—somehow whacked three inches off.

So my braids were a little shorter.

The rest of the shoot went smoother. I ran, and they took pictures. I had to change clothes a bunch of times because they weren't sure which color combinations would look best in the final prints. I really wanted a jacket—it didn't matter which color!

"I'm FREEZING!" I pointed to the snow-topped moun-tains in the distance. "Why are we doing this in January?"

"Welcome to the world of retail marketing, kiddo.

Gotta stay a season or two ahead of the game." Flip didn't look cold at all, even though he was wearing flip-flops, a tank top, and shorts. Very wrinkled ones.

We took a lunch break at one o'clock. Hot pizza and cheesy bread. Yum. But my hope to get out of there early shrank when I saw Fawn bring out more clothes and shoes. That meant more photos. Which meant me missing signups. I had to do something.

Smiley Bob was enjoying his pizza with my parents at a picnic bench in the middle of the track. I decided to ask one harmless little question:

"Um … Mr. Hansen? Do you think we could end the shoot at, like … two o'clock?"

Mean looks came from both of my parents. (I'd be in trouble later with them, but better them than with TJ.)

Mr. Hansen put down his pizza, brushed the crumbs off his hands and fished for his pocket watch (which all suit guys seem to have).

"Hmmm … let's see … two o'clock?" He looked at the time and then dropped the watch back in his pocket. He shook his head. "Impossible. I'd say we have at least three hours left before we wrap this thing up."

I let my shoulders droop down … really far. (I did that on purpose to add a little drama.)

"What's wrong Riley? Are you feeling okay? I suppose we could come back out here tomorrow morning if—"

"She's feeling fine. Plus, tomorrow's Sunday, and that

would interfere with *our* agreement." Mom shook her head and gave me an annoyed look. (Yep, I was going to be in trouble.)

Flip came over to offer some Oreos for dessert—whole ones this time.

"What's the Sunday agreement?" He was eating the cookies out of his pocket from earlier.

"That's when we go to church, so Swiftriver doesn't schedule any work for me."

"Ah. Got it." He was quiet for a few seconds as we walked back to the track to set up for our next set of photos. Very un-Flip like.

"So, Flip, where do you go to church? I go to Riverglen Community." More quiet. He set his camera on the tripod, got out a bigger lens from his camera case, and looked over at me a couple of times. I just kept staring at him with my arms crossed, waiting for an answer.

Flip sighed. "Uh, I don't. Church and I don't get along real well, so I don't bug it and it doesn't bug me."

"That doesn't make sense. You should try our church. We don't have any bugs at all. Well, maybe an ant or two in the kitchen."

Flip laughed and popped another de-iced cookie in his mouth. "Can I show up wearing this?"

"Sure." At least I hoped so. I tried to think if I'd ever seen anyone dressed like that at church, and the answer was ... never. But that didn't matter, did it?

"What if I looked worse than this?"

"I'm pretty sure that's not possible!" Fawn came out of nowhere to get that little jab in.

"Do you go to church, Fawn?" I figured it would be fair to ask her too.

She plopped her huge make-up bag down on the bench, unzipped it, and practically put her whole head into it, looking for who knows what. "Define *go to*."

Fawn is so complicated.

"You know, going to church every Sunday to worship God."

She pulled out a big brush and some blush, applied it to my cheeks, and lowered her voice so I could barely hear her. "I've been in churches for lots of weddings and a couple of funerals, but no—I don't *go to* church."

I suddenly felt confused. No church. Huh. I've been going to church since I can remember. I like going— well, except for the getting-up-early part. I asked Jesus into my heart when I was eight, got baptized, went to church camps and Christian concerts, and had friends all around me who all did the same things. I couldn't imagine what it would be like if I never did all that. I didn't know what to say.

So I didn't say anything. I started thinking about TJ, and the fact that *she* was going to be at church tomorrow in a really bad mood because of me.

Chapter 9

I've gone to Riverglen Community Church for my whole life. I started in the nursery with Miss Barbara, went to the preschool class with Miss Dolly, and just this last summer I graduated from children's church, where I've been since first grade. It's a little awkward now that I'm in seventh, since we don't have a middle school group. So I get to choose between going to the youth group class (which has twelfth grade boys with mustaches in it) or going into children's church as a "helper." The older teens in youth group look at me like I'm some kind of alien, and the kids in children's church look at me like I'm a rock star. So the choice isn't hard.

The other two seventh graders, TJ and Sean, come into children's church to help too. Sean brings me my favorite donut (chocolate with chocolate sprinkles) every week and says, "Riley, if you marry me someday, your last initial will be the shape of this donut." Sean's last name is O'Reilly, so I don't even care that he's nice and semi-adorable. I'm not having the name Riley O'Reilly.

"Riley, I've been looking all over for you. Here's your donut!" How did Sean find me? I was hiding from TJ in the nursery and pretending to organize the diapers. (Miss Barbara lets me come in whenever I want.)

A new text came in on my phone. From TJ. Great.

Git to parking lot asap.

Need 2 talk.

U cant hide u weasel.

Weasel? Oh boy, she was beyond mad.

"Sean, you have to come with me." I ran out of the nursery, and he followed close behind, because that's what Sean always does.

"Does this mean we're engaged finally?" I couldn't even think of what to say to that 'cause I was too busy figuring out how to survive the TJ attack.

We found the crazy-mad girl out in front of the church with her sister Breanne. (She's a senior in high school, which makes her friends with those hairy boys in the youth group.) I didn't see TJ's parents, so Breanne must have driven them. Too bad, I could have used the protection. I started to say something, but she came right at me.

"You said you'd be there. You said, 'no prob.' You lied."

"TJ, I can explain."

"Do you know who signed up to be on our team?

Rusty Peterson. Is that who you want playing shortstop this year? I'll die, Riley. Grounders go through her legs all day long."

"TJ, keep your voice down. You're embarrassing me." Breanne twirled her hair around her finger and looked around the parking lot for boys—like she always does.

"Hey, who's the cute homeless guy?" Breanne pointed to the bike rack. We all looked around. I couldn't believe it—there was Flip, parking an old, rusty mountain bike in one of the stalls.

"Oh, wow—that's not a homeless guy. That's my photographer." I waved. Flip looked messed up as usual, but at least his faded green t-shirt had sleeves (it did have a big bleach stain under his right arm, though). The shorts and flip-flops were the same ones as yesterday.

"Hey, Riley." He waved back and came over to join us. "Nice shoes." I was wearing the pink Rock Shocker hikers.

Thanks. These are my friends, TJ and Sean."

"And I'm Breanne." She said her name funny. Breeeeaaaannnee. Her voice sounded whispery and way too sweet. She shook Flip's hand and held it a little too long. I had to do something.

"Flip, I'm so glad you came! Are you hungry? We have coffee and goodies in The Well." (That's the name of our church coffee shop.)

"Starving. Lead the way, kiddo." We all walked Flip

through the foyer to The Well. Breanne stayed close to all of us, which is not what she usually does. She usually acts like we're invisible.

Flip was carrying a crumpled, brown bag.

"You didn't need to bring a lunch. We'll be done before noon."

"Oh, this isn't lunch. It's a little something for Brady."

"My brother?"

I didn't know Flip knew Brady.

"Of course. Do you know any other Bradys?"

Sean laughed. "No, there's only one Brady."

"Is he here?" Flip looked from side to side.

"I dunno. I don't keep track of where my brother goes."

"I saw him a little while ago near the boys' bathroom," Sean said. "He was all dressed up in aluminum foil. He's Knight Knute today." (I'll explain that later.)

"Well, Riley, can you give him this? It's one of my old cameras from when I was a kid. He was interested in seeing how real film works."

Confusing.

"So, you've actually talked to my brother? When?"

"We've talked plenty. Mostly when you're getting your hair all perfect for the shoots. He's a cool kid. Do I smell baked goods?"

Flip grabbed a plate and started piling on the muffins. I counted five. Not the minis, the big ones.

Breanne was still hanging with us like we were her

buddies. She looked at Flip's pile of muffins and grabbed her stomach.

"You know those are like a thousand calories each, right?"

Flip raised his eyebrows. "Really? A thousand, huh? That's great! I've been looking for more calories. Looks like I hit the jackpot." He shoved practically a whole muffin top in his mouth. "Mmm, blueberry! Want some?" He handed the bottom of the muffin to Breanne.

"Thanks." She took it from him and started eating it! This whole scene was just wrong.

"I'm outta here," TJ whispered. "Are you coming?"

We tried to sneak away, but Flip stopped us. "Hey, thanks for inviting me to church. It's been great. See you next Saturday for the cross-trainer shoot." Then he walked out the door, got on his bike (after stuffing the muffins in his shorts pockets), and pedaled away. I stood there, shocked. *This wasn't how this was supposed to work!*

"Yep, he's homeless." Breanne sighed as she watched Flip ride away. "But I like his dimples." Then she turned to me. "It was good of you to invite him to church so he could get something to eat."

I shook my head. "Well, it wasn't exactly what I had in mind."

Breanne twirled her hair and looked around the parking lot again. "Next time, you should invite him to the service. We could find him something decent to wear in the missions closet or something. I bet he cleans up nice."

I laughed as I thought of the old vests and musty dress pants that have been in the missions closet forever. The missions people don't even want them, so the church has been using them for costumes. I like Flip's clothes better.

"I don't care what he wears," I said. "I just hope he comes back."

Chapter 10

Brady's been wearing the "Armor of God" that we've been making out of aluminum foil in children's church. The pieces all look good, but no other kid wears them to church each week. (And no one else has to rename himself. He's only answered to "Knight Knute" for a couple of weeks now.) So far, we've made the Helmet of Salvation, the Shield of Faith, the Belt of Truth, and the Sword of the Spirit. I wasn't sure what we were going to make this week.

Mrs. O'Reilly (Sean's mom) is the children's church teacher. She's pretty calm considering we have a bunch of crazy, overactive kids in children's church. Sometimes I just sit in the back of the room and pray for them to calm down so I can concentrate on the lesson.

"By the time I count down to zero, I want everyone to be in their seat and listening."

Mrs. O. began to count down from ten. She got to three, and no one had calmed down yet. If I were her,

I'd just walk out the door and never come back. By zero, half the room was calm. By negative five (she goes below zero if she has to), one of the older girls yelled "SHUT UP," which was totally inappropriate, but it worked. Everyone was silent. Mrs. O. just grinned and held up a roll of aluminum foil.

"Boys and girls, today we're going to make the Shoes of Peace that come from the Good News. When we get dressed every day, the shoes we choose to wear are very important. If you're going hiking, you need hiking boots to climb on rocks and rugged terrain. If you're going to run, you need shoes that cushion the soles and heels so they don't get injured from all the pounding. If you're going river rafting, you need sandals that attach to your feet so they don't fall off when you go in the water."

TJ elbowed me in the side. "Sounds like a Riley Mae shoe commercial."

Mrs. O. continued. "For a Christian, our shoes are the Gospel of Peace. Whenever we go out, we need to take Jesus with us. Having Jesus in our hearts is the only way we can experience true peace. We need to walk in his peace every day, and then we need to share that peace with others."

Right then, Ben Matlock sneezed and a booger flew out of his nose onto his chair.

"Gross, Ben! Get away from me." Emily Fremont is always grossed out about something, so I'm not sure why she was sitting by Ben, since he tends to be gross a lot. Everyone else started laughing. Mrs. O. walked over to the craft table, picked up a tissue, walked over to the chair, and snatched the booger up. She continued talking like nothing happened.

"How many of you have friends or neighbors who don't know Jesus?"

Lots of kids raised their hands.

"Then you need the shoes of Good News! Let's all remember to be ready to share Christ with the people he brings into our lives."

Mrs. O. unrolled a big piece of foil and showed the kids how to shape it to their foot and then how to use a hole punch to make openings for lacings. I knew right away that Sean, TJ, and I would have to punch all the holes for the kids since their hands were too weak. It turns out we had to lace them all up too, since they had a hard time concentrating enough to thread the yarn through all the holes.

It took the whole hour to finish sixty shoes—thirty kids times two. I was so tired, I never wanted to see another foil shoe again.

Erin Fremont—Emily's five-year-old sister—asked me to make her shoes look like my hikers. "I like those, they're pretty!"

I got a pink marker and colored the foil. She loved that. Then I signed my name on the sides.

"Does that say Jesus?" she asked. "Cause that's what I want it to say."

Oops. She was right. That's what it should say. Why didn't I write that?

"I'm sorry, Erin. I made a big mistake. Let me make you a new pair of shoes, okay?"

"Sean, can you get me some more foil?" If only he wouldn't have been hogging the roll, I could have snuck a new piece.

"What for?" He looked down and noticed Erin's first pair of crumpled-up shoes.

"She spelled Jesus wrong." Erin's cute, but I wish she would have kept her mouth shut.

"Jesus?" Sean raised his eyebrows. "J-E-S-U-S? How could you get that wrong?"

"Just a little misunderstanding. Now hand it over." I grabbed the foil from him.

"You don't have to get nasty." Sean shook his head and walked away.

I felt terrible, but I didn't have time to apologize. I had one more pair of foil shoes to punch and lace. Ugh.

TJ came up behind me and breathed down my neck.

"Okay—so you wanna come over to my house after church? We could have lunch and figure out the softball stuff." She was still mad at me. I could tell by the way she had pulled her hair to one side and was twisting it tight. But the fact that she was inviting me over was a good sign. I just didn't know what I was going to do to fix our problem.

"Sure. But only if we can make brownies."

"Okay." TJ smiled a little. "Let's go check with your mom."

Sean stopped us on our way out the door. "Riley, I forgive you for being nasty." He smiled and brushed his blond bangs out of his eyes. "See you next week with your donut." It's nice that I never have to fix things with Sean. And it's cute when his hair gets too long and hangs over his blue, sparkly eyes. But I'm still not marrying him.

Chapter 11

"Four games? That's it? I need another brownie." TJ sank her teeth into another fudgy bite. We both have a thing about chocolate. If it's around, we eat it—all. There was only one brownie left (and it was just me and TJ eating them so far).

I double checked the Riley Mae shoe schedule. Yep, I was only going to be able to play four softball games—if I was even allowed to sign up for the team.

"My dad will totally let you sign up."

Mr. Thompson came into the kitchen looking for a brownie.

"One left? Are you kidding me? How long have these brownies been out of the oven—ten minutes?"

"You'll let Riley on the team even though she can only play four games, right?"

"Huh?" He bit into the last brownie. Rats. I wanted that one.

"I have photo shoots every weekend but four. TJ

thinks you'll let me on the team anyway, but I would understand if you didn't."

He licked his fingers. "Can you be at practices during the week?"

"Yeah—no prob."

"Well ..." He scraped some crumbs off the bottom of the pan and scooped them in his mouth. "I'll make you a deal. Bake another pan of brownies, and I'll let you on the team."

Yum, another pan. TJ started pulling ingredients out of the fridge.

"It'll be great to have you practice with us. In fact, you could be a real help to our new shortstop. She could use some of your fielding tips. I think you know her. Her name's Shari Peterson."

That would be Rusty.

TJ practically dropped the eggs. "But Dad, when Riley's there, Rusty could play another position, right?"

He shook his head. "Nah, it wouldn't be fair to ask her to change positions for four games. Riley—you can be a floater this year."

"But Dad—"

"TJ—this is between me and Riley. You just practice pitching and not whining."

Mr. Thompson grabbed a newspaper and headed out to the backyard. "Call me when my brownies are ready."

TJ grabbed an egg, wound up, and pitched it against

the wall! She has a little bit of a temper, but that still surprised me.

I grabbed a paper towel and rushed to the wall. "Nice strike. You wanna get grounded?"

"Hey, maybe I could get grounded from softball season. Then I wouldn't have to play with Rusty."

"She can't be *that* bad, or your dad wouldn't let her play infield."

"She's okay, but she's not you."

Unfortunately, Breanne came in the kitchen before we got the egg cleaned up.

"Wasting food? Not a good idea. Some homeless person could've eaten that. Speaking of homeless, Riley, tell me more about your friend Flip." She pulled up a chair as if she was interested in us or something.

"He's not homeless. He's my photographer."

"You've been to his house, then?"

"Why would I go to his house?"

"I know—especially if he doesn't have one."

TJ looked like she was going to throw another egg. "Breanne, why do *you* care?"

Breanne rolled her eyes. "I care about people!" She stormed out of the room.

"Only if they're male and cute," TJ said.

The new brownies made it out of the oven within the hour. Thankfully, we never heard from Breanne again, but TJ's dad did come in and eat half the pan.

"What about the end-of-the-season tournament right after school lets out? Can you play in that?"

I grabbed the calendar and flipped over to June. "Looks like that Friday I have … uh … well, it says here 'Half Dome hike.'"

Mr. Thompson nearly choked on his brownie. "Half Dome? The Half Dome in Yosemite?"

That was the only Half Dome I had ever heard of.

"They want you to hike that? You know how hard a hike that is? It takes like twelve hours, and you have to pull yourself up on cables to get to the top."

"I'm sure they're just going to take some pictures of me with Half Dome in the background."

"I hope so." Mr. Thompson looked relieved. "I don't think I'd let TJ do that hike yet. You girls are in shape but not that good. Plus … it's a little dangerous."

"Well, at least that's the day before the tournament." TJ sounded like she was finally getting the mad out of her system. "So you'll make it, right?"

"Yeah, I'm sure I'll be able to play."

"At shortstop?" TJ doesn't know when to give up.

Mr. Thompson crossed his arms. "Floater."

"Not fair!" TJ stomped her foot.

Luckily the eggs were back in the refrigerator.

Chapter 12

A month later, the first commercial for the shoes came out on TV—the one with the boys' baseball team and the cloud of dirt. It looked a little different than I thought it would, but you could really tell it was me when I took off the helmet.

Life got a little complicated after that.

All of a sudden, people were coming up to me saying, "Hey, you're that shoe girl." In the store, at the park, in restaurants, it didn't matter. Everyone knew I was Riley Mae now. Some kids were even asking me for my autograph, so I started practicing writing my name really fast, and of course, I dotted the "i" with a daisy. I also started carrying around different-colored permanent markers so I'd be ready. But then I thought that would seem too big-shot like, so I just carried one color—pink.

Even weirder than seeing myself on TV was seeing full-sized posters of me in sporting goods stores all over Fresno.

"Ewww, creepy," was all Brady could say.

Each Saturday in February was "Special Guest Appearance Day." It was my job to appear "wherever fine sporting goods are sold." At least that's what the ads said. I got to give out fun stuff to girls—like pink sweatbands and hair ties—and pump them up about the Riley Mae shoe collection. The displays at the stores were amazing—big daisy-covered walls full of softball and running shoes in just about any design or color a girl could want. And from what I could tell, a lot of girls wanted them. At one store, a couple of girls got in a little fight over the last pair of "Butter Ups."

One girl brought a pair of pink daisy cleats to her dad. "Can I get these ... please?"

"In your dreams. Let's go see what Walmart has."

The girl looked like she was going to cry and just left the shoes lying there on the floor. Why would her dad say that? They weren't going to find anything better at Walmart. I walked over to put the shoes away.

Even the shoeboxes were cute. Every box design matched the shoes. I put the shoes back in the box and stacked it on the shelf. This pair was called Crazy Daisy, but I noticed that the name was covered by the price tag, so I peeled it off so I could put it somewhere else on the box.

Then I noticed the price. One hundred and thirty dollars.

ONE HUNDRED AND THIRTY DOLLARS?

I turned to watch the girl continue to fight with her dad as they walked out the door. It was all clear now. And I suddenly felt sick.

Chapter 13

The shoes cost too much! If I didn't get them for free, I wouldn't even be able to afford my own shoes."

Bob Hansen smiled (of course) and nodded. I had my parents drive me to his office so I could complain. "Yes, they are a little high-end. That's because it costs more to make them so unique."

"But how are people supposed to afford them? People don't have that kind of money to spend on shoes that their kid's just going to grow out of." That's what my mom always tells me when I want an expensive piece of clothing.

"Lots of people are affording them based on the first few weeks' sales. We're actually very pleased." Mr. Hansen pulled out some papers that had graphs on them. Yuck—graphs. I pretended to look at them and under-stand, and then I plunked myself down on the chair.

"But that girl was practically crying. It caused her and her dad to fight."

"It's just business, honey." Dad rubbed his neck.

"Are *all* the shoes that expensive?" Mom asked Bob. "Can't Swiftriver make something cheaper?"

Mr. Hansen pulled out another stack of papers with sketches on them. "We are designing some flip-flops for the summer that will go for around forty dollars."

I pictured my flip-flop collection at home. Mom would never pay more than $4.99 a pair. Riley Mae flip-flops were going to be ten times more expensive. I'm not too good at math, but even I could figure that out.

"I can't do this anymore. I'm sorry, Mr. Hansen, but you have to let me out of my contract." I took off my "Butter Ups" and put them on his desk.

Chapter 14

My next "Special Guest Appearance" was a few weeks later at my own softball team's opening day ceremonies. Mr. Hansen didn't let me out of my contract, by the way. The whole time I was complaining, he just grinned. Then he told me that he really liked the way I was looking out for girls who couldn't afford the shoes and said he was going to talk to public relations about doing some giveaways or something like that.

I wish they had done that first thing on opening day. Instead, I had to stand in a booth filled with boxes of really expensive shoes with my name on them in front of all the girls I know and pretend that the best thing for them would be to beg their parents to buy them.

"So, which ones should I get?" TJ pulled out box after box and scattered the shoes on the grass.

"You should get the 'A-Okays.'" (Those were the ones with all the red Ks all over. TJ's a pitcher, and when you strike someone out, the scorekeeper puts a K in the box.)

"Oooh, good idea! Do you have them in size six?"

I grabbed a box from behind the table. She pulled two one-hundred dollar bills out of her pocket and asked if I had change.

"Where did you get THAT?"

"What?"

"That money!"

"It's just two hundred dollars. My grandma gave it to me for Christmas. I was saving it for something special. Don't you think Riley Mae shoes are special?"

I wanted to say no, but I really do think they're special—just too expensive. "Of course. That's cool you're buying some."

"Yeah, I know. I'm trying to talk all the girls on the team into getting them too."

"That would be fun! Hey—maybe Swiftriver could do another commercial with our whole team in it. I could ask Mr. Hansen—"

"Hey, Mom says it's time for your break and she wants you to take me to the snack bar for a burrito." Brady was waving money in my face and pointing over at Mom, who was sitting with TJ's parents under a tree.

"You're old enough to walk to the snack bar. Can't you go get *me* a burrito? I've been slaving away here for hours."

"I'm just saying what Mom said. But it's okay. I'll go tell her you said no."

"No, let's just go." I grabbed Brady's arm and dragged him all the way to the snack bar.

"Help! I'm being kidnapped by Riley Mae—the evil shoe queen!"

"Brady, be quiet. Someone from Swiftriver's gonna hear you."

"I don't care about Swiftriver. I wish they never existed. They're ruining my personal life."

"What personal life? The one where you walk around the house all day imagining you're someone important? You should thank Swiftriver for getting you out of the house. Oh yeah, but you do the same thing no matter where you are, so who cares?"

Brady took off right as we were getting to the front of the line. The kid just didn't make sense—I thought he was hungry. I watched him go sit on the bleachers and swirl his shoes around in the dirt.

"Can I help you?" The lady at the snack bar looked a little annoyed. I noticed that a huge line had formed behind me while I was messing with Brady.

"No thanks, I think I changed my mind."

"Then step aside, please."

"Uh, sure. Sorry."

Now what? I looked over at Brady again and saw that Flip had arrived with some kind of scary snack for the two of them. I hoped it wasn't the dreaded pocket jerky. Okay, so he was taken care of. I got back in the snack bar line.

"What do you think you're doing in this line?" Fawn appeared out of nowhere. She was wearing a pink flowery dress and white sandals and was carrying a ridiculously huge straw bag.

"Getting a burrito. I'm starving."

"Oh no, you're not going to eat that junk. Nothing but empty calories here. Follow me."

She grabbed my arm, and this time I was the one being dragged. I didn't like it any better than Brady.

"Why are you telling me what to eat? You're just my makeup girl."

Fawn reached into her bag, pulled out a box, and handed it to me.

"You don't need a makeup girl anymore since your mom won't let you wear makeup. So now I'm your personal assistant. And apparently, you need assistance picking healthy food for yourself. I thought you were an athlete. Don't athletes know better than to stuff their faces with snack bar burritos?"

I opened the little cardboard box Fawn handed me. An apple, a turkey sandwich, and some string cheese. Yeah, this was a better choice. But it was missing something.

"No chocolate?"

Fawn reached into the straw bag and pulled out a fun-sized bag of peanut M&Ms.

"Here. Ten calories each. Portion control is everything."

"Gee, thanks." I was beginning to wish I had my makeup girl back and no personal assistant.

"Now, eat up, because you're giving away a free pair of shoes in about fifteen minutes. I'll meet you over at the booth."

All day long we had been asking girls to put their names in a jar for a drawing for a free pair of Riley Mae shoes. I kinda hoped that girl from the sporting goods store would be here. I hadn't seen her yet. It would have been cool to pull her name out of the jar. Then she could return her Walmart cleats, and she and her dad would both be happy.

As I walked back to the booth, I spotted Rusty Peterson. She was digging in the cleat exchange barrel.

"Hey Rusty, I hear you're joining our team this year. It'll be great having you play shortstop."

Rusty pulled her head out of the barrel and grinned at me. "Thanks, Riley. I'm really happy about it too. That is, if I find some cleats that fit."

Rusty stood half a head taller than me, and she had long legs, which would make her fast at running the bases. I figured she got her nickname from her hair color, but why did every girl I know have beautiful, long straight hair except me? I pulled out a hair band and put my out-of-control mop in a ponytail.

I looked down into the barrel. "What size do you wear?"

"Eight. I've got big feet. No one ever brings those to exchange."

We pulled out every pair. Seven-and-a-half was the largest size in the barrel.

"Why don't you come over and try on some Riley Maes? Taylor was hoping our whole team would have them."

"Uh, well … no offense or anything. I really like the shoes, but … it's just not in our budget right now. See, my dad, well … he lost his job about a year ago."

I swallowed hard.

"I'm so sorry."

"It's alright. We moved into a cheaper apartment last month, so our bills are less now. I just hope he gets something soon so we don't have to move in with my grandma in Oklahoma."

I felt like my fancy cleats were glowing, and I wanted to hide them. I had so many pairs. Unfortunately, they were all size six-and-a-half so I couldn't give any of them to Rusty. Then I got an idea.

"Hey, did you put your name in for the free shoe drawing?"

Rusty's eyes brightened. "No, I didn't know about it."

"Come with me."

I took her over to the Riley Mae booth and grabbed an entry blank.

"Quick, fill this out. You could win."

Rusty scribbled her name and address on the paper and I folded it up and stuck it in the jar. I really wanted to have her fill out a bunch of slips, but that would have been cheating. One would have to be enough.

"Come back in fifteen minutes," I told her.

"Okay, but I'm gonna go grab those seven-and-a-halves out of the bin just in case. They're the closest to my size and maybe they're stretched out or something."

"Okay."

I just knew she wasn't going to have to worry about that.

I didn't need to check my watch for when the drawing started because my new personal assistant hunted me down.

"C'mon, Riley. Drawing time." Fawn had added a floppy hat to her outfit of the day. Bob Hansen joined her and began tapping on the microphone to see if it was on. Thump, thump, thump. It was.

"Good afternoon, everyone. We want to thank you for letting Swiftriver be a part of your event today. Our company takes pride in bringing you the very best shoes for anything you like to do outdoors! The name of the game today is softball, and we have the privilege of giving away a pair of cleats from our new Riley Mae Collection for girls. And to do the honors, we have a special guest. Your own hometown spokesgirl—Riley Mae!"

Everyone clapped, which was nice, but I didn't have time to enjoy it because Mr. Hansen stuck the microphone in my face. I didn't know what I was supposed to do with it, so I looked at Fawn. I was hoping for some really quick personal assisting. She whispered instructions.

"Say thank you and that you're glad to be here. Then pick a slip from the jar and read the name."

Yeah, I guess I could have figured that one out if it hadn't been for the attack of the nerves. My stomach was all tied up in knots. I saw Rusty leaning up against a tree toward the back of the crowd. Had all these girls filled out slips for the drawing? What were the odds I would pick Rusty's name?

I cleared my throat.

"Thank you, everybody. It's great to be here today in good old Fresno." It was *my* voice I heard, but it was like I was listening to someone else.

"Let's see who's going to win a free pair of Riley Mae shoes!"

I reached in the jar and felt around for Rusty's name. Why didn't I fold an edge down or something? I guess that would have been cheating too. I grabbed a handful of papers and then started letting go of one at a time.

God, please let me pull out Rusty's name.

I finally decided on one slip of paper, and my hands shook as I unfolded it. A sweat drop fell down from my forehead onto my thumb. Gross. I hoped nobody saw that. My eyes blurred and then a familiar name jumped off the page. I took a deep breath.

"The winner of the shoes is … Taylor Thompson." I looked up and saw Rusty grin and shrug. She pointed to the seven-and-a-halves and gave me a thumbs-up sign.

Taylor ran up to me, shrieking. "Can you believe it? It's like you had best friend radar or something! Come help me pick out which pair I should get!"

I sighed and followed her to the table. I wondered if I could talk her into a pair in size eight.

Chapter 15

TJ wore her free Crazy Daisy shoes to the first day of practice. I wore my old cleats from last year. Mom said that was against the contract, but since I knew Rusty would be wearing the stretched out seven-and-a-halves, I couldn't let her be the only one wearing old shoes. Just as I thought, everyone else was wearing Riley Maes.

TJ noticed right away. "What's up with the shoes?"

"I dunno. I just missed my old cleats."

"Whatever." She rolled her eyes and ran out to the pitcher's circle.

"Okay girls, let's take some infield." Mr. Thompson stood at home plate with a bat and a ball, ready to hit some grounders.

"Riley, since all our bases are filled, why don't you be a floater between short and second today?"

TJ frowned as her dad hit the first grounder right up

the middle to her. She snagged it up in her glove and fired it right back to Stacie Ferguson, our catcher.

The next grounder came the shortstop's way, and Rusty bent down to make the play. The ball bounced kinda funny just as she got ready to grab it, which sent it up and over her glove ... right through her legs. I watched her shoulders drop as I snatched the ball and threw it back.

"Sorry. I guess I'm not quite warmed up yet."

TJ gave me an intense stare.

"It's okay, Rusty. That one took a nasty hop." Mr. Thompson tried to encourage her.

He hit a few more grounders to the other infielders and then sent some fly balls to the outfielders. Rusty did a great job being a relay person from the left fielder. Every time she threw the ball, it hit dead center in the player's glove.

"You're so accurate. Do you practice that a lot?" I wanted to encourage her too.

"Not really. I just have good aim, I guess."

Mr. Thompson started the second round of grounders, and when the shortstop's turn came around again, I found myself praying that Rusty would make a fantastic play so that TJ would stop glaring.

It didn't happen. The next grounder came hard at Rusty and whizzed right through her legs again. TJ slammed her glove down in the pitcher's circle. I hoped

Rusty didn't see that. I looked over at her, intending to say something to cheer her up, when I noticed that she was a little shaky. She grabbed her head and bent down on one knee.

"Everything okay?" Mr. Thompson put down his bat and started out to check on her. I ran over and got there first.

"I can't believe I keep missing those," Rusty whispered to me.

"Are you sick?" Mr. Thompson helped Rusty up on her feet and looked into her eyes. I watched a tear slide out of her right one.

"Hey, coach, can we take a quick break? You're wearing us out." I tried to take the attention off of Rusty.

"Break already?" TJ had now joined us—with no sympathy. "Haven't we had, like, a nine-month break?"

Mr. Thompson looked like he was thinking hard about something. Then he turned and called out to all the girls. "Five-minute break! Grab a drink, and then be ready for sliding drills."

All the girls ran in from the field and started fishing in their backpacks for their water bottles.

Rusty didn't, though. She walked slowly over to the drinking fountain near the dugout—the one with the nasty tasting water. (It tastes just like you swallowed a mouthful of pennies.)

Something was majorly wrong about that. All the rest

of us had our sport bottles. I looked around for a back-pack that might have been Rusty's but I didn't see one. She probably forgot to bring it. So I ran over to see if I could find out what was up.

"If you drink that, you'll gag." I warned her too late. She had already taken a big gulp from the fountain. It was entertaining watching her face, though.

"Eww."

"Did you forget to bring a water bottle? I only have this one, but you can share it with me. I don't have too many germs." I held the bottle out to her. She grabbed it and sipped down at least a third of the bottle.

"Thanks, that tasted much better."

"Did you forget to bring a drink? I didn't see your backpack anywhere."

"Uh, no, I didn't bring one today."

"You'll never make it through one of our practices without water. Mr. Thompson really works us out."

Rusty swallowed hard, and I noticed that her face was really pale.

"Are you sure you're not sick?"

"No."

"Cause you look sick to me."

She turned and walked away from the drinking foun-tain, farther away from the team.

"Rusty, what's wrong?"

She stopped walking and put her head down. I stepped up next to her.

"I'm not sick."

"Then, what?"

"I'm ... hungry."

I was relieved. I could do something about this.

"Oh, well you've come to the right place. I stuffed my backpack full of granola bars this morning, and I'd be glad to share."

Rusty looked up at me and smiled.

"When was the last time you ate?" I expected Rusty to say breakfast, 'cause I know sometimes I miss lunch for dumb reasons.

It was a simple question, meant to make small talk as we returned to where my backpack was, but the answer shocked me somewhere deep inside.

"Uh ... let me think—"

She had to think about it?

"I guess it was Sunday dinner."

My jaw dropped a mile at least. This was Wednesday afternoon!

I didn't know what to say. I dove into my backpack, grabbed a granola bar, and tore it open. I handed it to Rusty.

"Eat. Now."

She did. Next I pulled out an apple. She started to eat that too.

"Okay, girls, I want to see you out on that field!" Mr. Thompson walked over to me and Rusty.

"Everything okay over here? Rusty, you look better." He grinned.

I answered. "Yep, we're all better now. Thanks for the break, coach."

He nodded and turned to run back to the field.

"Thanks for the food, Riley. When I bent down to field those grounders, I got a little dizzy. Maybe I'll do better now."

I just stared at her. She stared back.

"Does this happen a lot?" I couldn't let her go yet.

"What?"

"You, not eating. Are you anorexic?"

"No. I mean yes."

"Huh?"

"No, I'm not anorexic. Yes, sometimes I don't eat."

"Come on, girls!" Mr. Thompson hollered. He was standing over at home plate with the rest of the team.

"Why not?"

"Riley, Rusty! We're waiting on you!" There was no mistaking TJ's annoyed voice. She had her hand on her hip.

"We better go ..." Rusty broke into a run. I was bugged that she didn't answer me, but I was happy to see that she looked better.

But I got worse.

My concentration went out the window. My mind was so caught up in the Rusty situation that I totally forgot the coach's instructions on what we were supposed to do next.

Who doesn't eat for three days?

During our sliding drill, I forgot to slide and got tagged out at second base during a routine play.

"Afraid to get scraped up? That's not like you." TJ pulled me aside in the line for the next drill.

"Nah, I was just thinking about something else."

"Thinking about how we need a better shortstop?" TJ smirked. She was really getting on my nerves.

"Rusty's a good player. You should give her a break."

"What, are you best friends now?"

"No, I'm just saying that you need to give her a break. Not everyone can be perfect like you." Oops. That was mean.

Thankfully, TJ and I have been friends for a long time. We've said mean things to each other before and then we say we're sorry and forgive each other. This time would be no different ... I thought.

"I liked you better when nobody knew your name." She turned, huffed off, and didn't talk to me for the rest of the practice.

Chapter 16

No one should go without food for three days. That night at dinner, I tried to go without a second roll and I couldn't. I was just too hungry from practice. Then, an hour after dinner, I had a bowl of cereal.

"Mom, Riley's eating all the cereal again." Brady's always telling on me.

"She's growing, honey. She needs fuel."

I stuck my tongue out at Brady. Then he poured himself his own bowl of cereal.

As I was munching, I thought of Rusty. She was growing too, but she was going without fuel for some reason. The next day, I decided I was going to fix it so she never had to do that again.

But I basically never see Rusty at school. Or at least I've never noticed her being around. Usually, TJ and I are hanging out, and we get talking about stuff and don't look for other people at all. But on Thursday morning,

I decided I'd keep an eye out. I really wanted to get an answer to the question I'd asked Rusty the night before:

Does this happen a lot? You not eating?

I just needed to keep TJ from talking my ear off.

That turned out not to be a problem. As soon as she saw me coming toward her at the lockers, she whipped a U-turn. Then she looked back over her shoulder, put her hand out, and said, "Don't talk to me."

So I didn't. Instead, I looked for Rusty.

She wasn't hard to find. She was standing in front of her English classroom.

"Rusty!" I ran over to finish our conversation from the day before.

"Hi, Riley. Wow, I never see you at school."

"Yeah, I know."

"Nice shoes." I was wearing some purple Riley Mae cross-trainers.

"Thanks."

There was an awkward silence. I wanted to jump back into our conversation from practice, but I didn't want Rusty to feel bad. So I just stood there like a dummy.

Finally, Rusty spoke.

"I told you that my dad hasn't had a job for a year, right?"

"Yeah."

"Well, he does get an unemployment check, which pays some of the bills and buys us food."

"That's good."

"But sometimes the food runs out before he gets his next check. That's what happened this month. It's not a big deal."

I still didn't know what to say.

"He's getting paid again on Monday, so we'll go shopping then."

This was Thursday. Now I had something to say.

"Are you telling me you don't have anything in your house to eat until Monday? That's horrible!"

Rusty looked at the ground. "We have a box of rice and some gravy. I think we're having that tonight. It's okay."

"No, that's NOT okay! You're gonna faint if you go that long without food."

Then I remembered the game.

"The first softball game is Saturday. How are you going to have energy to play?"

I also remembered that I wouldn't be there on Saturday. I was flying to Arizona with Swiftriver for an appearance at Arizona State University. The college softball team was putting on a workshop for the girls' teams in the area, and it was going to be this big deal with entertainment, food booths, demonstrations, and companies that sell stuff, like Swiftriver.

"Riley, please don't tell anyone what I told you, okay?"

"Why not? There are people who can help."

"No! My dad would be so embarrassed. He's trying hard to take care of us. People might not understand. He's afraid I might get taken away from him."

"Why would that happen?"

"I don't know. He just said it could."

That would be horrible. I couldn't imagine being taken away from my parents just because they didn't have a job.

"Okay. I won't say anything. But I have to do something. You need food."

The bell rang then. So annoying.

Rusty opened the door to her class. "I'll see you at practice."

I bought an extra burrito at lunch and looked all around so I could give it to Rusty. I couldn't find her. I didn't think it would stay good until practice, so I ate it. I was full by the third bite, but I couldn't bring myself to throw it away, knowing Rusty was hungry. So instead, I felt like a pig.

I had to fix this problem for Rusty. All I needed was a plan—by the end of practice.

Chapter 17

Practice went better than the day before for Rusty. I snuck her a water bottle, a granola bar, and a banana before we started.

No grounders went through her legs this time.

TJ looked as annoyed as ever and still refused to talk to me.

I still couldn't concentrate. Luckily, Mr. Thompson put me in the outfield, so I didn't need to pay attention as much. I can catch fly balls all day long without giving it much thought.

What should I do about Rusty?

Practice was about to end, and the next day after school I was flying out to Arizona. And I wouldn't be back until late Saturday night. I had to get Rusty some food without anyone knowing about it.

Super Walmart! I have to get there. With Rusty.

The new Super Walmart was just around the corner from our practice field. I had been there with my family just a week ago, and I was ashamed to think of all the money I wasted at the grand opening sale. I couldn't even remember what I bought that day. I felt in my pocket for the twenty dollar bill I brought with me to practice. It was all the money I had left. It would have to be enough.

I could ask Mom to drive Rusty home and stop at the Super Walmart first. But for what?

"Riley! Watch out!"

Our center fielder, Katie Bleavins, yelled and pushed me out of the way at the same time so she could catch the fly ball that was coming straight for my face.

"Whoa—I didn't even see that. Thanks, Katie."

"Yeah, no problem. Quit staring at your shoes so you don't get killed."

Had I been staring at my shoes?

"Okay, ladies, that's a good sign that we've probably had enough. Run ten laps around the bases and then you're done for the day." Mr. Thompson took off running to lead the team. I like that he works out with us.

TJ was out in front, right behind her dad. Usually we run together, but she didn't wait for me. I figured she was still mad, so I ran with Rusty. I needed to tell her the plan anyway.

"Rusty, is your dad picking you up from practice?"

"Uh, no. We don't really have a car right now, so I'm walking home. It's only a few blocks."

That was good news. Well, sort of.

"Okay, so here's my plan. I'm gonna ask my mom if she can drive you home, but then I'll ask her to stop by Super Walmart first so we can go in and get something we need for school. A special folder or something . . ."

"Okay, but why would we do that?"

"Because you need to buy some food! And since you won't let me tell anyone—"

"Oh, I get it now. But how am I going to afford that?"

I pulled out my twenty. Rusty shook her head.

"No. I won't let you spend your own money on me."

We were huffing and puffing pretty hard right then since we were on about our fifth lap.

TJ came around and lapped us. "Making plans for after practice? Well, don't invite me, I'm busy." She sprinted by.

I ignored her. I had bigger problems at the moment. This was urgent. "Rusty, you *have* to let me do this for you. Please. You need energy, especially for the game on Saturday. I know it's not much, but we can pray that God will help it last until Monday."

"God? What does *he* have to do with it?"

TJ came around again. "Some people need to pick up the pace!" And off she went.

"So, are you in or out? If not for you, think of the team! You want to be on your game on Saturday, don't you?" That worked.

"Okay. Let's do it." Rusty started to sprint. I struggled to keep up. She really is a good athlete.

"Great. Now I just have to figure out a way to keep my mom from coming into Walmart with us."

"Thanks, Riley. I really appreciate everything you're doing."

"No prob."

We finished our tenth lap when TJ was already getting into her dad's car.

She yelled back at me. "Have fun in Arizona. I'll text you the score of our game when we lose." She slammed the door. Wow, she was *still* mad.

Just then, Mom pulled up. Brady was with her. I'd never been so glad to see him.

Chapter 18

I don't wanna go in. Please don't make me go in!"
For once, Brady was helping me out, without even
knowing it.

Mom shook her head. "I wish you would have told me
you needed these folders earlier. I would have left Brady
home."

"It's okay, Mom. We can go in by ourselves. We're old
enough now, don't you think?"

Mom parked our mini-van as close to the exit as she
could get. "Okay, hurry up. You've got fifteen minutes
before I storm the building. And don't talk to anyone you
don't know."

"What about the checker-outer?"

"You know what I mean."

Rusty rushed out of the car so fast she forgot her
backpack. We needed that to put the groceries in, but
since I couldn't tell her anything in front of my mom, I
just grabbed mine.

"Riley—come back here!" Why was Mom calling me back?

"What? I was just hurrying like you said."

"You need money for the folders, right?" Mom reached into her wallet and pulled out a five-dollar bill. "Go ahead and buy Rusty's too."

That would help. Now we could spend the whole twenty on food.

"Oh, thanks."

Rusty was almost at the grocery aisles by the time I caught up to her.

"What should we buy?" I didn't know anything about buying groceries. Not where anything was or how much anything cost.

"Peanut butter and crackers, string cheese, some apples, mac and cheese ..." Rusty obviously knew what to do. She'd even thought to get a hand-basket to put it all in.

The clock was ticking.

"You go get some granola bars and nuts." Rusty pointed over at the produce aisle. "I'll grab some oranges."

We joined back up at the checkout. Rusty frowned as we looked at the filled-up basket. "I don't think we have enough money," she said.

"I hate this! You need everything in here to make it to Monday."

Chapter 18

"It's okay. Let's just put the oranges … uh … um … no. We'll put the nuts back. Yeah, the nuts cost the most."

I wanted to cry. This was all Rusty would have to eat for the next three-and-a-half days.

The total came to $19.33. Whew, just made it.

"Okay, somehow we're gonna have to transfer this to your backpack in the car without my mom or Brady seeing."

"What about the folders?"

"Oh no! We're running out of time!"

We whipped around to go back to the school section and almost knocked down the Walmart greeter.

We picked up the first folders we saw and made it through the checkout and to the car with two minutes to spare. That was important, because when my mom says she's going to storm a building, she really will.

"Did you get what you needed?" Mom looked back at our bag of folders and frowned. "Riley, we have some just like that at home."

"Oh, uh … sorry. I forgot. Well, thanks for taking us anyway."

Mom shook her head.

Now we had to figure out the food exchange. For some reason, Brady just wanted to stare at us for the whole ride to Rusty's house, so it wasn't going to happen the way we planned. Ugh, he's so annoying sometimes! I

took out my phone, typed out a memo, and showed it to
Rusty:

Switch backpacks.

Don't let Brady see.

Will trade tomorrow.

Rusty nodded. She looked at Brady. He looked at her.
Then he looked at me. Ughh!

I erased my memo, and then my phone buzzed. A
new text.

"Who's that?" Brady wanted to know. Ah, a
distraction!

"I'll look later." I pretended not to be interested. Brady
can't stand that.

"What if someone needs something right now?"

"They can wait."

He was falling right into my trap. "Lemme look.
Please?"

I knew it could be a big mistake, 'cause who knew
what was in that text. But I had to switch backpacks.

"Okay, but don't mess my phone up." I gave it to him.
He looked at it for a moment. That's all we needed. Rusty
grabbed my backpack handle, and I grabbed hers.

"It's from TJ. She says, why are you hanging out with
E-girl? Who's that?"

"None of your business."

"But you let me look at it."

"So what? I don't have to tell you what it means."

Unfortunately, E stands for error, and now Rusty knew that TJ thought of her as Error Girl. Great.

"Mom, Riley's being mean!"

"I am not. But I will be if you don't stop bugging me."

"Knock it off, you two! I hear enough of this stuff at work. Can't I get a little peace around my own family? Sorry about them, Rusty."

"It's okay, Mrs. Hart."

"So, where do we drop you off?"

"Just a few more blocks. South Street Apartments."

"O ... kay." Mom's eyes narrowed.

I found out why when we got to the apartments. This was the bad part of town.

Rusty lives here?

"You can just drop me off on the corner." Was she kidding?

"Oh no. I'm walking you in. Kids, you come with me too." Mom got us out of the car, locked it, and did her usual "area scan" before we went up the stairs to Rusty's apartment.

We got to Rusty's apartment, and she took out her key.

"Isn't anyone home?" Mom continued her scan. Brady tried to run down the stairs, but Mom grabbed him by the shirt sleeve. "Stay near me, buster."

"My dad should be getting here any minute. It's okay, I've stayed by myself before." I was hoping my mom would be so concerned about Rusty staying alone that she wouldn't notice that she had my backpack.

"Okay, but I want to go in with you. Then I want to hear you lock the door as we leave. Use all the locks."

So that's what we did. The apartment was clean, but it didn't have much in it. A couple of chairs and a TV, a filled-up laundry basket in the corner, and some boxes stacked along the wall.

"We just moved in so we're not unpacked yet." Rusty looked embarrassed.

"It looks fine, honey. Very cozy. I love the new carpeting." Mom knew how to make someone feel better. The place did have nice carpet.

"Here's my phone number. You call me if you have any trouble after we leave, okay?"

"Thanks Mrs. Hart. I'm sure I'll be fine."

After hearing all the locks click, Mom led us back to the car.

"I'm glad you're Rusty's friend." Mom patted me on the back.

We made it all the way home and into the living room before Mom took me aside.

"Make sure you get your backpack from her tomorrow."

Chapter 19

Sometimes I wish my mom wasn't a cop. I don't know why I try to sneak stuff by her. It never works.

"My backpack? I don't know what—"

"There's my family! I was getting worried." Thankfully, Dad interrupted me just as I was getting ready to really stretch the truth and probably get grounded. He was rolling a suitcase in from the garage.

"Arizona tomorrow—you ready, Riley?"

"What do I have to do to get ready?" All I could think to do was pack ... I guess.

"What time does your flight leave tomorrow?" Mom was already in the kitchen getting things out to make dinner.

"As soon as we can get to the airport after school."

"That doesn't make any sense. Don't you guys have airline tickets with a departure time listed?"

Something wasn't right here.

"Aren't you coming, Mom?"

"I have to work, honey, and Brady has science camp. But you'll have Dad and Flip and Fawn."

"You're going to love the private jet," Dad said.

"A private jet?" Mom looked surprised. "Why didn't I know about that?"

Dad patted me on the shoulder. "Pretty nice way to travel, huh?"

Mom's eyes narrowed again.

"Swiftriver has a private jet? That's extravagant. Didn't you say they're a fairly new company?"

"About three years old. Lots of companies have jets."

"I know, but not new little companies. Swiftriver seems to have quite a bit of capital too."

"What's capital?" I asked. They were leaving me out of the conversation again.

"Stuff. They have a lot of stuff for a company just getting started. Don't you think that's unusual, Bart?"

"I think you're just naturally suspicious. Not everyone needs to be investigated."

"Well, I think it sounds fun to have a whole jet to ourselves," I said. The only other time I'd been on a plane was when we went to visit my aunt and uncle in New York. We were squished in a back row by the bathroom, and we couldn't even recline our seats.

Mom just kept looking at my dad. "Just how long have you known Bob Hansen?"

"Three years. Relax. You're off work right now." Dad went over and rubbed my mom's shoulders. When she gets like that only he can calm her down.

"Riley, you need to go up and pack a day's worth of clothes. The weather report says it's going to be hot. Make sure you take all your shoes since you don't know which ones they'll want you to wear."

"Okay, Mom."

I started to head up the stairs when I heard Mom say to Dad, "Maybe I *should* go with you. I could cancel one of my meetings and Brady could . . ."

Dad interrupted. "Everything's going to be fine. It's a shoe company, Lynda. Quit trying to make something out of nothing."

"Bart, you know I never do that. Ever."

Chapter 20

The private jet was really private: only me, Dad, Bob
Hansen, Flip, Fawn, and these two other Swiftriver
employees, Justin and Al. They cracked me up. They
kept joking and punching each other—kinda like
brothers. They work for the company doing lots of things
like setting up equipment. It was their job to set up our
Riley Mae booth at the college and haul in a hundred or
so boxes of shoes.

"Best job I ever had," Al said, as he finished setting
up the overhead canopy at our booth. "Where else do
you get to travel in a private jet, set up a few things,
and then go relax and get tan?" He grabbed a folded-up
lounge chair and went looking for—I guess—some sun.

"Hey, that's my chair!" Justin ran after him, grabbed
the chair, and they fought over it for awhile.

"You're wasting my tanning time," Al yelled. Flip was
circling the guys, taking all kinds of pictures during

their little scuffle. He has a whole slideshow on his computer of hilarious Justin and Al moments.

Bob Hansen came running over to the booth. "Everything looks great. I hope you're ready, Riley. They're expecting about eight hundred girls at this clinic. Make sure they get excited about the shoes!"

I wasn't sure if I was still excited about the shoes. I felt a little scared too—this was the biggest event I had been to yet. I still didn't like that the shoes were so expensive, and I was worried about Rusty and the softball game back home.

"Can I go get something to drink?" I had to ask Fawn's permission to leave the booth—that was an order from my dad, who had gone to the college library to find a way to print out some forms or something for Bob Hansen.

Fawn was arranging the shoe display to make it look nice. Justin and Al had just plunked the stuff down.

"Well …" she looked at her watch and then at the display, which wasn't quite ready. "I can't really leave just yet, but …" She looked over toward the snack shack which was only a little ways away.

"I guess you could go over and get something without me. You're a big girl." She smiled and handed me a twenty dollar bill. "Get four water bottles. No soda. See if they have any fruit."

I really wanted to get a lemonade, so I did. Fawn had just said no soda. And lemonade had fruit in it. If she didn't like it—tough. Arizona was hot and lemonade was necessary.

I turned away from the snack bar and bumped into a young man dressed in nice clothes. One of the water bottles fell to the ground. He reached down to pick it up.

"Oops, sorry about that, young lady."

As he handed me the bottle, he smiled.

"Hey, aren't you Riley Mae from Swiftriver shoes?"

He was dressed like some of the reporters I had seen at different Swiftriver events.

"Yeah, that's me."

"Would you like a hand with that?"

"Uh, sure. I guess." I pulled my lemonade out of the drink carrier and handed him the rest. This was the kind of guy Breanne would act silly around.

"I can't believe this—I'm from *Diamond Dust*, the girls' softball magazine. Have you heard of it?"

"Oh, yeah! My friend TJ has a subscription. We get all kinds of good tips from that magazine."

"Well, that's great to hear. Hey, your boss and I have been trying to get together with you for an interview about the new Riley Mae shoes."

"Oh, so you're a reporter?"

"Yep, I'm kinda new. This is one of my first on-location jobs. I'm a little nervous."

I could totally relate to the guy. "Yeah, I'm pretty new to all this too."

He set the drinks down on the ground. "So, how long have you worked for Swiftriver?"

"A few months. I went to my Dad's office to try on some shoes and they liked me, so they offered me a contract."

"Wow, that was lucky." He got out a pen and notepad and started to write some things down.

"Well, I didn't really know what a contract was—if I did I probably wouldn't have done it."

"Why not?"

"Too much work. And I have to miss playing softball, which I love—and now my best friend's mad at me."

"Sorry to hear that. But I bet the people at Swiftriver are nice to work with. The company is based in Fresno, California, right?"

"Yeah, that's where I live too. And the people are very nice. They take good care of me and make me laugh." I pointed over to the Swiftriver booth. Flip and Fawn were doing what they normally do—Fawn was working and Flip was goofing off, taking pictures of Fawn working.

"So those two are Swiftriver employees?" He wrote some more.

"Flip and Fawn—my photographer and personal assistant."

"Are they married?"

"Are you kidding? Those two can't stand each other. Well … in a funny sort of way."

Fawn looked up from her shoe display and yelled my name. Then she started to walk over. The reporter picked the drink caddy up off the ground and handed it to me.

"Well, it was nice meeting you, Riley. I hope we can get a formal interview soon."

"Sure—thanks."

"Riley! How long does it take you to get drinks?" Fawn was huffing and puffing in her purple high heels. She shielded the sun from her eyes as she looked back toward the snack shack.

"Who were you talking to?"

"Oh, he was just some reporter from *Diamond Dust* magazine." I put my hand over the top of my drink so she couldn't see it was lemonade.

"A reporter?"

"Yeah, he said he was new."

"Did he show you a press ID?"

"What's that?"

"A pass that shows he's a reporter. What was his name?"

"Um, I don't know. He didn't say."

"But he knew *your* name." Fawn grabbed her forehead and started pacing back and forth. What was the big deal? Didn't Swiftriver want some publicity?

"Well, yeah. He said he's been trying to get an interview with me and Bob."

Chapter 20

Fawn shook her head and didn't talk to me as we walked back to the booth. I figured I had broken some law of the contract by the way she was acting. Maybe I'd get fired and I could go back to playing softball and being normal again.

"Flip, get over here. Riley, tell Flip what you told me."

Flip grabbed his camera off the tripod and quickly walked over.

"Did you do something to upset your personal assistant again?" Flip had that smirky face that he usually has when he's teasing Fawn.

"Yeah. She doesn't like that I was talking to a reporter."

Fawn put her hand on her hip. Flip frowned, which he never does.

"A reporter? Man or woman?"

"Man."

"What did he look like?"

I had to think about that. I didn't want to tell him that the man was young and cute and that TJ's sister, Breanne, would want to date him. So I came up with something close to that.

"I guess he looked a little like you. Only his clothes were neater." I laughed, thinking that would lighten things up.

It didn't.

Flip shook his head. "You shouldn't talk to reporters without an adult. What kinds of things did he ask?"

Now I had to really think. What *did* he ask? And what did I say? Sometimes my mouth just runs.

"Well, he wanted to know about you two. If you were married. Wouldn't that be funny?

I thought Flip and Fawn would laugh at that, but instead they exchanged wide-eyed glances.

"Did he say anything else?" Flip asked.

"He asked how long I've been working for Swiftriver, and if Swiftriver was in Fresno."

Fawn looked like she was going to faint. "Did you tell him?"

"Tell him what?"

Flip put his hand on Fawn's shoulder. "Never mind. It's no big deal, Riley. We're just a little stressed about your safety. You have to be careful. Not everyone is who they say they are. I'm sure this guy was a real reporter who wasn't thinking straight."

"He did say he was new to the job. I'm sorry, you guys. I didn't think it would matter."

"It's my fault for letting you go off on your own." Fawn shook her head some more.

"Hey—could we not tell my parents about this? Especially my mom. She'll freak if she finds out I talked to a stranger."

Bob Hansen arrived on the scene. "Are you guys ready

to get some people excited about shoes?" He looked around at our serious faces. "What's going on? Don't like the heat?"

Flip grabbed the lemonade out of my hand and took a big sip. "No—it's great! Riley got me lemonade, so now I'm happy."

"Oh good," Bob continued. Then let's get out there and meet some nice people!" He started out toward the crowd that was gathering and directed them to the booth.

Fawn whispered in my ear. "You stay right here for the rest of the afternoon. I don't care how nice the people are—don't tell them anything. Just smile. If you do, your parents won't find out a thing. And ... I'll get you another lemonade."

That was all I needed to keep my mouth shut.

After about two hours, Justin and Al came back to take down the booth. They were both red as tomatoes.

"Boss says we're leaving early. Good thing, since Al ran out of tanning lotion."

Al punched Justin in the arm. "Yeah, 'cause you used it all. Get your own next time, dude."

There were still lots of people around, and even though most of the shoes were gone, we still hadn't done the giveaway yet.

Bob Hansen ran up to the booth. "Riley, have you ever seen shoes disappear so fast? Even those college girls loved them! We might have to think about making some bigger sizes."

It was fun to meet some of the college softball players. They were so nice—they kept coming up to the booth to get my autograph. I asked for their autographs too, since I want to be a college softball player someday—when I'm not a shoe girl.

"Why are we leaving so soon? We haven't even done the drawing yet."

"Gotta get the jet back home—another group from the company needs it. We've done a good job here promoting the shoe line, so it'll be okay. I'm sure you want to get out of here, right?" Mr. Hansen smiled.

Yes, I did. I was still feeling a little stupid about my mistake earlier with the reporter, and I didn't know what I would say if I saw him again. It was a good time to get out of Arizona.

"Why don't you just give away a pair of shoes to whomever you want, okay?"

I didn't have to think about that for more than a second.

"Sure. Thanks, Mr. Hansen. Do we have any size eights left?"

"Check with Justin and Al. They'll be loading up what's left."

I prayed for one pair of eights. Right about the time I said "Amen," a text came in from TJ:

Chapter 20

We lost.

Like I thought.

Guess who messed up?

Chapter 21

TJ came over to my house Saturday night after I got home from the airport.

"I threw a bad pitch, and the girl hit it over the fence. We lost 5–4." I was relieved it wasn't Rusty who messed up, but I really felt sorry for TJ—she *hates* to lose.

"Don't worry about it too much. It's just one game, and if you weren't such a great pitcher, the score could have been higher."

"I would have done better if you were playing short. I get nervous with Rusty there and it distracts me."

"You know, Rusty is a better athlete than I am. She's quicker and taller, so she can get to balls faster. She just needs to build her confidence."

"Whatever. How was Arizona?"

"It was okay. The jet ride was fun. Something weird happened with a reporter, and I sort of got in trouble for talking to him. But that's just between you and me. Don't tell anyone else."

TJ grinned and leaned closer to me.

"And I have a secret for you."

"What?"

"Breanne wants to find out more about Flip."

"That's no secret."

"I know. But she's planning to come to your photo shoot this weekend, and she wants to follow him home—*if* he has one."

"That's not nice."

"Yeah, but it's interesting. Don't you want to find out where he lives?"

"I guess."

"So are you in or out?"

"What do you mean?"

"Do you want to check it out with us? I'm going to go too. We don't have a softball game this weekend. We could tell your mom that you're coming home with us, and then we could follow him."

"I don't know. Sounds like a dumb plan. Why don't we just ask him where he lives?"

"Rileeeeey ... come on. It'll be like solving a mystery. You can be Nancy Drew." (TJ and I always used to pretend to solve mysteries when we were smaller. We took turns being Nancy and George.)

I didn't want to do it. But then I thought it could be a way to get back to normal again with TJ. We hadn't had any fun together since the whole shoe thing started.

"Okay. I'll do it. But if we get caught, I'll just pretend I didn't know what you guys were doing, and I'll say you forced me to come. I don't want Flip mad at me."

"We won't get caught."

All week I worried that my parents might find out. I also wondered if it could get me fired from my shoe contract. If that were the case, maybe it would be a good thing to get caught.

At least I didn't worry about Rusty starving during the week. Her dad got his unemployment money on Monday, so they were able to go buy a bunch of food. I also got to give her a little gift at practice on Tuesday.

"Hey, guess who won the shoe giveaway in Arizona?"

She shrugged.

"You." I handed her a box of size eights in a brand-new Riley Mae design—the Teal and Steals. (They have sparkly teal lightning bolts.)

"No way. I can't take these."

"You have to. You won them, and I'm not allowed to give them back. Anyway, they're your size, and you steal a lot of bases, so they're perfect."

"How did I win them if I wasn't even there?"

"God worked it out."

"What does *he* have to do with it?

Why did she keep saying that? God has everything to do with stuff like this. Didn't Rusty know that? I was silent for a minute, and then I remembered something Mrs. O'Reilly said during her Armor of God lesson:

"For a Christian, our shoes are the Gospel of peace. Having Jesus in our hearts is the only way we can experience true peace ... we need to share that peace with others."

I believed that, and I wanted to share it with Rusty, but I didn't have a clue what to say, except:

"Well, he loves you a lot."

Rusty looked down at the ground and shook her head.

"I'm not so sure about that—for me, I mean. But it's okay. I think I understand why. But I'm glad you've been so nice to me."

Why would Rusty think that God doesn't love her?

I still had no idea what to say.

So the rest of the week when I wasn't worried about following Flip, I was trying to figure out what to say to Rusty about Jesus.

"Mom, what would you say to someone who isn't sure Jesus loves them?"

Mom pulled up a barstool and answered right away. "I'd tell them that they're crazy. He died on the cross to prove it."

I asked my dad too. "I'd tell them about Christmas. How he left heaven and became a man so that he could be our Savior."

I even asked Brady. "I'd tell them that I *know* he loves

me. So that proves that he loves *them,* cause hardly anybody even likes me."

Crazy, but Brady's answer made the most sense to me. And then I felt bad for my brother but happy for him at the same time, since at least Jesus is his friend.

But I still didn't know exactly what to say to Rusty.

So I got back to worrying about following Flip.

The Swiftriver photo shoot was at Woodward Park on Saturday. I was supposed to model some cross-training shoes while working out on the fitness course that surrounds the park. It was really cold again, but at least it was sunny. Everything was going great until Breanne and TJ showed up after lunch.

"We told your mom we'd take you home." TJ tried to do a secret wink, but she wasn't very good at it. She just looked like she had something in her eye.

"Need eye drops?" Flip pulled a bottle out of his pocket.

"Check the expiration date on those." Fawn laughed.

Breanne came strolling over to us wearing—a dress?

"Hi, everyone." She was walking with her hands on her hips, like she was a model or something. Tilting her head back and forth too. "So, Flip, how's work going today? Is Riley cooperating?" She patted me on the head like I was a baby.

"She's a pro now. No trouble at all," Flip said.

"We're giving her a ride home later. Would you like one too? I noticed you have your … uh … bike again."

Fawn laughed some more as she walked away.

"No thanks, I'm good. I like riding—it's good exercise."

Breanne walked over and put her hand on Flip's shoulder this time.

"Are you sure you don't want a ride? It's awfully cold out here, and you're not wearing much." That was true. It was the faded t-shirt again, with shorts and flip-flops.

"Nah, I'm good. Really. Plus, you might try to kidnap me."

"Huh?" Breanne tossed her head again. Gross.

"Whenever I get around a bunch of ladies, they never want to let me go. Too much charm, I guess."

TJ and I cracked up. Breanne frowned and stomped over to sit on a bench. Score one for Flip.

As soon as the shoot was done, Breanne was all over us again.

"Riley, don't forget we're taking you home, honey." Honey? She gestured to me to hurry up. On her way over to the car, I saw her pick something up off the picnic table where Flip had all his equipment. Whatever it was, she stuffed it in her purse. There was no turning back from the plan now.

Chapter 22

W hat did you steal off Flip's table?" I barely got
the car door closed before I let Breanne have it.
"That's not a good way to get him to like you."

"You shush. I just took one of his camera lenses. How
else will I have an excuse to follow him?"

"You could just tell him you're obsessed." TJ flipped
her head back and forth. "Oh, Flip, are you cold? You look
so cute with all those goose bumps all over your legs."

We both laughed and Breanne punched TJ in the
arm—hard.

"Owww. I'm telling Mom."

"No, you won't. Then you'd have to tell her what we're
up to, and you'll get in trouble too."

I saw Flip coming up on the right side of the car on his
bike.

"You guys, here he comes." Breanne looked off in the
other direction so he wouldn't see her face. He rode right

past the car and through a red light at the intersection. We had to wait.

"Oh no—I can't lose him!" As soon as the light turned green, Breanne took off. "He's moving really fast."

We followed him for about thirty minutes until we started coming into the business area of town.

"He can't live here. Even homeless people don't live in these areas." Breanne had been keeping a few cars between us so Flip wouldn't know he was being followed, but he'd just pulled into the parking lot of a strip mall, so she stayed in the street and drove next to him.

"That's the Swiftriver business office," I said. "He's probably stopping there to drop off stuff before he goes home."

TJ checked her watch. "We don't have a lot of time. Mom's gonna wonder where we are."

"Well—*do* something about that. Text her and tell her we're going to the store or something." Breanne would not be deterred from her mission.

"I'm not texting a lie."

"Fine. We *will* go to the store then! Just do it, TJ."

We watched Flip open the door to the office and take his bike inside. We waited a long time for him to come out.

"Breanne, we gotta go," TJ pointed to her watch again.

"No way." Breanne scowled at TJ, and then she threw open her car door. "I'm going in."

"No you're not! What are you going to say?" I knew this was a dumb idea.

"Just come on, and don't you two say anything. I don't want you messing things up."

"I'm not going in there. I don't want Flip knowing I was following him too."

"It's too late Riley, you're in deep. Your mom will kill me if she finds out I left you out here in a car alone. Get out now."

Mom would kill me anyway if she found out anything about this little plan. So I got out and followed.

We walked up to the door, and I prayed it would be locked so Breanne would give up and take us all home. But the door was open, so Breanne walked in. TJ and I followed behind her. The place was dark, and it looked like nobody was there.

Then we saw a light come on down the hall.

"Come on," Breanne whispered. We heard a toilet flush. Then a door cracked open. We ducked behind some desks, and I felt like my heart was going to pound out of my chest.

Flip came out to the main office area where we were hiding and turned on some lights. He didn't see us because we were still behind the desk. He was wearing pajama bottoms and no shirt. The weirdest thing was that his hair was combed. Breanne sighed.

We watched him lock the front door with a key and

then turn a bolt from the inside—I wondered if we were going to be able to get out now. Then he turned off the light and walked back down the hall.

"He doesn't look like a guy who's just dropping stuff off." TJ was sounding a lot like Nancy Drew now.

"Maybe he's going to work awhile in his office and he's just getting comfortable," I said. "You know how Flip is with clothes."

"Well, let's find out." Breanne popped out from behind the desk and marched down the hallway.

"Hello? Hey ... is anyone here?" She was blowing our cover! TJ and I caught up to her, though, 'cause we didn't want to be left alone in the dark.

She knocked on a few doors that led to the room where Flip was. Then we came to his office.

The name plaque on the door said *Flip Miller—Swift-river Photography*. I never knew his last name was Miller.

"Hello?" Breanne pushed open the door to the office. It was all over now.

We walked in. But Flip wasn't there.

"Let's get out of here," I said, and I reached for the door handle.

Breanne plunked down on an old couch in Flip's office—well, after she had moved a bunch of clothes to make some room.

"I'm staying. He'll show up soon. I have to give him his lens." She pulled the lens out of her purse.

I looked around a bit. The place had a refrigerator, a microwave, a couple of bean-bag chairs, and a coffee table, which was stacked with empty pizza boxes and some dirty coffee mugs. Newspapers were on the floor, and several pairs of flip-flops were piled in a corner. It didn't look like a work office at all. Flip's bike was parked in another corner, and his equipment bag was hung from a hook on the wall.

Next to the bag were pictures of kids. Lots of pictures.

TJ noticed the pictures too. "Who do you think these kids are?"

Breanne got off the couch and walked over to the wall. "Okay—this is weird."

I started counting. I got to one hundred and twenty when there was a huge crash from outside the office. I wanted to hide, but before I could, Flip came in.

"Are you here to kidnap me?"

Chapter 23

Breanne grabbed her throat. "Oh, good, it's you." Flip was holding a big box of books. "Sorry if that crash scared you. This slipped out of my hands out there." He set the box down and looked at us. "But I shouldn't be apologizing for scaring you—since you broke into *my* office. So, should I call the police, or are you going to tell me what you're doing here?"

Flip didn't look like the happy Flip I usually work with. I knew this was a bad idea.

"Who are all these kids?" TJ was still counting over at the picture wall.

"Is this your camera lens? I found it on the ground at the park." Breanne handed the lens to Flip. "I hope you don't mind that we followed you here. We knew you'd need it."

Flip nodded his head. "Yeah, that's mine. Funny—I sure thought I left it with the rest of my lenses on the picnic table."

"Some kid at the park probably moved it." Breanne was a good liar.

"Yeah—I'm sure that's what it was." Flip grabbed the lens from Breanne and put it back in his equipment bag.

"You have 200 pictures of kids on your wall. Who are they?" TJ wouldn't let up.

Flip went over to the pile of clothes, picked up a wrinkled shirt, and put it on. He turned away from us, rubbed his temples, and then turned back around.

"I sponsor them."

"What's that mean?" TJ asked.

Flip walked over to the wall of pictures. "I give money to help take care of them. They're all from different countries." He began pointing to different rows of pictures. "These are from Africa, these are from South America ..."

Suddenly, I thought of Maritza—a little girl my family sponsors from Honduras. We send thirty dollars a month to help her with education and medical needs. I started to do math in my head, which never works out, but I did realize that sponsoring two hundred kids meant a lot of money.

"Wait—you don't sponsor all of them every month, do you?" I asked.

"Well ... yeah. Lots of kids need help these days."

"I know, but that's like ... a bunch of money."

"Six thousand dollars a month. Seventy-two thousand dollars a year." Breanne obviously knows more math than I do.

"It's worth it." Flip pointed to some more kids. "These are from Romania—"

"Is that why you live in your office? No money left for a house?" Breanne looked around the room. "Where do you sleep, anyway?"

He pointed to the couch. "There. Hey—what did you guys do with my pillow?"

He rummaged through the clothes pile and pulled it out of the bottom. "Aw—it fell on the floor. I hate dirty pillows." He brushed it off, threw it on the couch, and flopped down.

"See—just as comfortable as a bed."

We all just stared at him.

"Look—I work a lot of hours. Makes no sense to have a house when I'm here all the time. It's a waste of money. Bob's okay with it—he likes having me here to keep an eye on things."

"It was Breanne's idea to follow you." TJ just couldn't keep her mouth shut.

Breanne gave her a really dirty look. I was pretty sure TJ wouldn't make it home alive now.

Flip laughed. "It's okay. Hey, I know I act really weird. I knew you guys were following me anyway. Got any more questions?"

Breanne just stared into Flip's eyes. "Ummm, do you

want to come to church tomorrow? We could share a muffin."

He stared back. "Maybe."

TJ rolled her eyes. "Breanne, we have to get home before Mom freaks out."

The stare was broken as Breanne looked at her watch.

"Oops ... yeah. I guess we better go. Come on, kids."

Kids?

Flip walked us down the hall and opened the office door. I took a step outside, but then Flip grabbed me and jerked me back in.

"Hey, I thought you wanted us to leave."

Flip put his finger to his lips and pointed to a silver sports car that was parked across from the office entrance.

"One of your friends?" He whispered to Breanne.

"No. I didn't bring anyone else."

Flip told us all to hide behind the desk we had been behind earlier. My heart really started racing then. At least when we were hiding from Flip, we knew he wasn't dangerous. Why was Flip so freaked out about this car? Was there some danger we didn't know about?

Then we all heard an engine start, and the car squealed its tires out of the Swiftriver parking lot.

"Coast is clear," Flip said. "You can come out now."

"Maybe that was Mr. Hansen," I said. I remembered him driving some sort of fancy car.

"No, it wasn't Bob."

"Probably just some punks racing around." TJ was still playing Nancy Drew.

"Yeah, rich punks probably." Flip kept watching out the door, and didn't let us out for a few minutes.

"We've really got to go." Breanne was finally looking really nervous about the time.

"Okay." He opened the door and looked around. "Just get right in the car and go straight home. And—this visit is going to be our little secret. I don't want a bunch of people to know I live here. And Riley doesn't want to get fired for snooping. So not a word to anyone, you girls got me?"

I certainly wasn't going to tell anyone. I actually didn't care about getting fired, but that would be the least of my problems if my mom found out what we had been up to that night.

Chapter 24

Flip didn't come to church the next day, but Rusty did. Rusty *and* her dad. I was so distracted watching for Flip that I didn't even notice they were there until we were being dismissed for children's church.

Rusty caught up with us in the lobby.

"So where do seventh graders go?"

"There's a teen group in the next building over." TJ obviously didn't want Rusty coming with us.

"Don't go there," I said. "They're all in high school. You can come with us and help in children's church." I gave TJ a dirty look.

Mrs. O'Reilly was thrilled to have a fourth helper. "We're making the breastplate of righteousness today. The kids are going to need lots of help."

"The what?" Rusty looked around at all of us. I didn't have a clue what to say.

"You'll see." Sean came to the rescue, as usual. "So,

Rusty, who invited you to church?" I wished he hadn't asked that question.

"Uh, well, Mrs. Hart called my dad and invited us. He made me come. I'm glad I saw you guys, or I would have felt really stupid being here."

I never thought that being at church would make someone feel stupid. I guess I've just gone for so long it feels normal. I can't believe I never thought to invite Rusty.

While Mrs. O. talked about the Breastplate of Righteousness, I was still thinking about the Shoes of the Gospel of Peace. I realized that I wasn't ready to share the gospel with Rusty, or anyone else. I'd been wearing all sorts of shoes, but when it came to the ones that really mattered, I was really messing up. Some shoe girl I was.

"Do you have a Bible?" I decided that would be a good thing to ask. Rusty looked up from fitting Ava Zimmer with a foil breastplate.

"No. Do I need one to go to church?"

"No, but you should have one. There's a lot of good stuff about God in it."

"Like what?"

I was speechless … again. Where was Sean when I needed him?

Ava spoke up. "There's good stuff like how God made

the world and the animals and the trees …" (But she said it like this: wuwold, animos, and twees.)

" … and God made the boys, but then the best part was when he made the girls."

That's when Sean walked up.

"But the girl came from the rib of the boy." Sean pointed to his side.

"Very funny," Rusty said. "That sounds like a little kid story." She was right—it did sound a little weird.

"No, it's true!" (But Ava actually said twooooo.)

Rusty stood up and admired Ava's finished breast-plate. "If you say so."

Ava ran over to the corner table, grabbed a book, and handed it to Rusty.

"You can have *my* Bible." She opened to one of the first pages. "Right there. See—God made the girl." She pointed to a picture of Eve. "She's pretty, like you."

"That is a nice picture." Rusty handed the Bible back to Ava.

Ava frowned. "No, I gave it to you—for keeps."

So that's how Rusty got her first Bible ever: *The Young Reader's Beginner Bible*.

"Lucky!" Sean said. "I wish mine had cool pictures like that." He grabbed it from Rusty and started flipping through it.

Ava grabbed it back from Sean and handed it back to Rusty.

"It's hers!" (But she actually said huzz.) Then she ran off.

Out of the corner of my eye, I saw Rusty smile and hug the Bible to her chest.

Chapter 25

"You think we should invite Bob, Flip, and Fawn over for Easter?" Mom was flipping through the calendar. "Bart, do any of them have family close by?"

"I don't know. We don't talk much about that kind of stuff."

"Riley, do they ever mention anything like that to you?"

"No. Not really." (I was pretty sure Flip wasn't going to bake a ham at his "home" at the Swiftriver office, but I couldn't say anything about that.)

"Well, I think it's a good idea. All they can say is no, right?"

They probably would say no. But I didn't want to disappoint my mom, so I went along with it.

"Yeah, sure. Let's do it."

"Great. I'll talk to them on Saturday after the photo shoot."

"Another one?" I was hoping I would get to play softball next week. Nope.

"One more before spring break. This one's at the community pool—for the flip-flop collection."

I looked out at the wind whipping through our trees in the front yard. "Brrrr."

"Quit your complaining," Mom said.

"Okay, but I'm not wearing a bathing suit."

"Unless they say so." Dad wagged his finger at me.

"Ugh!"

Chapter 26

I had to wear a bathing suit. At least it was a one-piece—but it didn't make me any warmer. No one was at the pool except us crazy people. I guess that's what models for catalogs have to do—freeze in the winter for summer ads, and roast in the summer for winter ads.

"Umm, I'm turning blue. Do you think we could get some hot chocolate or something?" I plopped down on a lounge chair and shivered to make my point.

Fawn pulled out a thermos and poured me a cup.

"No marshmallows?"

She pulled some out of her bag and dropped in a handful.

"Flip, I'm starting to like Fawn better than you." I grabbed a towel to put over my lap.

"She does have her good days."

Fawn poured Flip a cup of hot chocolate too.

"This is all real cozy, but can we go inside or something? People wear flip-flops inside too."

"And some people *only* wear flip-flops." Fawn pointed down at Flip's feet.

"You *do* have regular shoes, right?" I remembered the pile of flip-flops at Flip's office.

"Hey, I work for a shoe company. I have all kinds of shoes. I just like when my toes can breathe."

"That's how he got his nickname, you know." Fawn put her hands over her mouth after she said that—like she was letting out some kind of big secret.

"Your name's not Flip?" Now that made sense. Who'd name their kid Flip?

Flip chugged the last of his hot chocolate, handed the cup to Fawn, and gave her a weird look.

"Thanks a *lot*, Fawn."

Then I started to think. Who would name their kid Fawn? It's a pretty name, but unusual, for sure. Was that a nickname too?

"So, what's your real name, then?" I was talking to Flip, but I looked back and forth at both of them.

"Tarzan." He beat his hands on his chest and let out a big yell. "I'm surprised you never figured that out before this." He grabbed his camera and leaped off the chair. "Let's finish up inside where it's warmer. Whaddya say, Jane?" He grabbed Fawn's hand and pulled her out of her chair.

Tarzan and Jane. Whatever.

Chapter 27

Mom had been waiting in the warm car instead of freezing with me during the photo shoot.

"Riley, hurry up and get in! I want to catch Fawn and invite her to Easter dinner. She's about to take off."

We both watched Fawn throw her stuff in the trunk of her car and drive out of the parking lot.

"She can't get away. I wanted to talk to her today." Mom stomped on the gas pedal. "Let's follow her."

"That's weird, Mom. Can't we just call her?"

"Don't you want to see where she lives?"

If I didn't know better, I'd think I was in the car with Breanne.

"I guess."

"Good. I brought her some homemade cookies. I thought I'd sweeten the Easter deal a little. People can't say no when you give them cookies."

We followed Fawn for about fifteen minutes into an area where the rich people of Fresno live. Fawn's car pulled into the driveway of a beautiful house with big trees and a walkway up to the door that seemed a mile long.

"I wonder if she lives with her parents," I said.

"Probably not. But maybe she's married to a really wealthy guy." Mom just stared at the house.

"Fawn never mentioned being married."

We pulled up to the curb in front of the house and just missed Fawn as she drove into her garage and shut the automatic door behind her.

"I guess she didn't see us. Now what?" I asked. I hoped Mom wouldn't say we were going in.

"We're going in."

We waited in the car for a few minutes so Fawn would have time to unload things from her car and actually get in the house to hear the doorbell. At least we weren't breaking in on her like we did with Flip.

We walked fifty-three steps to get to the front door. There was this really fun woodpecker doorknocker that I insisted on using, but after a few minutes of pecking—no answer.

Mom tried the doorbell, and a really nice song began playing.

"I think that's Bach," she said.

The song played to the end, but still no answer. So we rang the bell again.

"Well, we know she's here. Maybe she's in the bathroom." Mom wasn't giving up.

Fawn finally opened the door just a crack.

"Oh, wow—it's you guys. I thought I heard someone out here. I was way in the back of the house. Is everything okay?"

Just then, a man came running by, chasing a really big, mean-looking dog. The leash was on the dog's neck, but the handle was dragging behind. The dog ran up Fawn's driveway.

"Get in here—quick!" Fawn opened the door wide and waved us in.

I practically dove into the house. Mom followed behind.

Fawn slammed the door and took a couple of deep breaths. "I can't stand big dogs. That one looked like it could chew us all up."

Mom and I watched out the window as the man grabbed the dog and put him in a silver sports car across the street.

"Well, he's gone now," I said. "He just drove off."

Fawn looked relieved. "Did you see what the guy looked like?"

"Young," I said. "But I was too busy looking at that scary dog to notice anything else."

"I got his license plate number." Mom pulled out a notepad and wrote the number down.

Fawn closed the window shades. "Well, next time he better hold onto that leash or I'm going to report him to the homeowner's association."

Mom and I just stood there for a moment, staring. The woman we were looking at sounded like Fawn, but she didn't look like Fawn at all.

She was wearing sweatpants, and her hair was pulled back in a ponytail that was sticking out of a baseball cap.

And all the makeup was gone.

And she was wearing Riley Mae running shoes.

Fawn looked down at her shoes, then back up at us.

"Uh, I was just getting ready to work out."

"We're sorry to interrupt. I wanted to give you these in the parking lot, but you got away too fast." Mom handed her the cookies.

"Oh ... um ... thanks."

"Can I use your bathroom?" I asked.

"Riley, that's rude." Mom frowned as she glanced my direction.

"But I really have to go."

"It's okay, Mrs. Hart," Fawn said. "It's down the hall, third door on the left."

So off I went. I didn't really have to go to the bathroom, but I did have to go down the hall to check the place out. Breanne and TJ would be proud.

Mom, however, would be mad if she knew what I was up to. I couldn't help myself. Fawn in sweatpants just made me super curious. In fact, the stuff inside her house was kind of strange too. I couldn't really put my finger on it, except to say that the whole place wasn't Fawn-like. Fawn is "foofy" (that's the word my dad uses to describe super-girly girls), and this house was definitely not "foofy."

I snooped in the bathroom but didn't find any clues. It just looked like a normal guest bathroom with nice nature pictures on the wall. No "foof" there either. I really wanted to find Fawn's bedroom and look in, but I was afraid I'd get caught, so I headed back down the hallway. As I did, I noticed a framed picture hanging on the wall. It was a photo of Fawn and Flip—Flip was wearing a suit and his hair was combed—and some other guy who looked a little familiar. I think it was one of the Swiftriver employees, but I wasn't sure.

"Are you coming?" Mom called from the end of the hallway. "We have some hungry guys at home wondering where we are, I'm sure."

"Yeah." On my way back, I noticed a door to one of the rooms was open. I pretended to trip over my feet and fall down right in front of it so I could have a quick peek inside. It was a huge workout room with a treadmill, a stationary bike, and weight machines. It also had a big TV hanging on the wall.

Fawn met me in the hallway.

I got up off the ground. "Wow, you must like to work out," I said.

"I have to keep up with you sport-os. You think climbing up Half Dome is going to be easy?"

"What are you talking about?"

"Those cables are going to be tough, so I've been pumping a little iron."

"Cables? Wait—are we really climbing all the way to the top? I thought we were just taking pictures by it."

Fawn laughed. "How do you think we're going to get by it?" She punched me in the arm. "You better get in shape, sister."

"Riley—come on! We've wasted enough of Fawn's time." Mom was using her gruff police voice.

"Hey Fawn, how come your house isn't foofy?"

Fawn crossed her arms. "Huh?"

"Riley—out!" Rats. The visit was over. I followed Mom out to the car.

"Is she coming for Easter?" I asked.

"Yeah. I told you the cookies would work."

Chapter 28

The next softball practice went a little better. TJ was talking to me now after the whole Flip adventure, and we were all starting to adjust to my role as a floater instead of shortstop. Rusty was doing great in the field—now that she had some food in her stomach.

"I guess I really am climbing up to the top of Half Dome after school lets out."

Mr. Thompson's eyes bugged out of his head.

"Holy smokes, girl. You better be careful."

"Don't get hurt—you're playing in the tournament the next day, remember?" TJ has a one-track mind.

"Is that the only reason you don't want me to get hurt? Thanks a lot."

"No, but it's the best reason."

"You're so mean."

"Yep, I am." She threw her glove at me and started running laps around the bases. I didn't want to run at all, so I just sat down on the ground.

Rusty came and sat down next to me.

"Guess what? Your shoe company gave my dad a job."

"Really? That's so awesome!"

"Yeah, he's going to work in the manufacturing plant, and a little in shipping. He'll probably be sending out Riley Mae shoes every day."

"I hope so! Did he already start working?"

She shook her head. "Not until after Easter break. He had to get a background check and fingerprints first."

"Really? To ship shoes? Wow."

"It's okay. They're paying him pretty good money."

"They should, with what they charge for shoes. Hey, maybe you'll get to ride in the private jet sometime. It would be nice to have someone my age come with me on a trip."

"That would be great. Hey, Riley, can I ask you something?"

"Sure."

"Well, I've been reading *The Young Reader's Beginner Bible*." We both laughed.

"Anyway, I was reading about Jesus dying on the cross."

"Oh."

"And I was wondering—why did he do that? I mean, it seems like he could have gotten away since he did all those other miracles. I don't get it. What happened? That's not a good ending—him dying and all."

"Did you read any more after that?"

"No, I had homework."

"Girls—why are we sitting when we should be running?" Mr. Thompson nudged me in the back with a bat.

"Tired," I said.

"Too bad. Do it anyway."

So we got up and ran our ten laps. We didn't have a chance to finish our conversation, but I did yell something to Rusty as I was getting in the car.

"Keep reading!"

"Okay," she yelled back.

Chapter 29

Somehow my mom managed to get everyone to agree to come to Easter dinner. Not just Bob, Fawn, and Flip, but also Rusty and her dad. I was glad, since Rusty's dad hadn't started his job at Swiftriver yet and they may have been low on food again.

"I'm looking forward to the job," Mr. Peterson, whose first name is Rob, told Dad. "But I feel a little nervous knowing the big boss is coming to dinner."

Bob Hansen hadn't arrived yet, but I assured Mr. Peterson it would be okay.

"Mr. Hansen's cool. He never stops smiling. I kinda forget he's the boss most of the time."

Rusty and I went outside to throw some balls while we waited for the rest of the company to arrive.

"So, now you know Jesus didn't stay dead," I said. Rusty and her dad had come to church that morning and heard the Easter message.

"Uh-huh. He resurrect—what's that word again? I don't think it was in the *Beginner Bible*."

"Resurrected. He came back to life."

"That's it. I still don't get why he had to die, though."

"Well, he died for our sins."

"But *why* did he have to do that?"

I missed the ball Rusty threw to me and had to chase it back to the fence. While I was chasing, I tried to think of a good answer to her question.

God, help me. I want to wear the "Shoes of Good News . . ."

I picked up the ball, turned, and ran back to where Rusty was standing.

"The Bible says that we all have sinned and fall short of the glory of God. That means we're separated from him unless our sins are paid for." (Wow, that memory verse from Sunday school just sorta popped out.)

"Well, can't we just do some good deeds to make up for our sins?"

"Hmmm. That's a good question. How many good deeds do you think you'd have to do?"

Rusty laughed. "Oh, about a thousand million."

"Yeah, me too."

Rusty shook her head. "I don't believe that. I'm sure you are way better than me."

"Hardly."

"But your mom's still here."

"What?"

"Your mom didn't leave. Mine left."

I couldn't believe what I was hearing. *Rusty's mom left her family?*

"Where did she go?"

Rusty stopped throwing. "Don't know. I just know she left because of me."

"That can't be true."

"I have proof." Rusty put down her glove and pulled a wrinkled-up piece of paper out of her pants pocket. She handed it to me.

"I don't think I should look at this."

Rusty shrugged. "Why not?"

"I dunno. Seems private."

"Go ahead. I've been wanting to talk to someone about it."

My hands shook a little as I unfolded the paper. The nice writing didn't fit with the message:

Dear Rob,

I'm sorry to have to break your heart again. You know I try not to. Please forgive me, but I have to leave. I can't do this anymore — it's too hard. I knew this would happen if we had a child. You and Shari will be better off without me.

Love, Cheryl

P.S. I'll miss you forever. Please don't try to find me.

A wave of sadness washed over me, and my eyes got teary.

"Rusty, where did you get this?"

"It was in some boxes I was unpacking at our apartment."

"Have you asked your dad about it?"

"No—and I'm not going to."

I folded the paper back up and handed it to her. "You should tell him you found it. He could explain what happened. How old were you when your mom left?"

"I think I was around five."

Mom yelled out the kitchen window. "Girls! Everybody's here. Come in and get cleaned up for dinner."

"I'm not hungry anymore, are you?" I grabbed my glove and ball and headed for the house.

"I'm starving." Rusty patted her stomach. "We have food in my house right now, but Dad and I are terrible cooks. I've been saving room for this meal."

Brady came out, all excited. "Hurry up! Dad says I can show my egg trick when everyone gets to the table."

"Egg trick?" Rusty raised her eyebrows.

"Who knows?" I said. "It's Brady. Could be good, could be a disaster."

It turned out to be both.

Chapter 30

Fawn's outfit was the best yet: a white dress with big yellow polka dots and shoes to match. Her hair was pinned up, with just a couple of perfect curls coming down the side of her neck. I wanted to flick them with my finger just to see if they were real. I would have if we weren't sitting around the formal table. I was surprised Flip hadn't done it yet. He caught me looking at the curls and made a motion like he was pulling one down so it could *boing* back up.

Flip wore a wrinkled outfit I hadn't seen before. An orange shirt with a little yellow chick on it. Below the picture, it said, "This chick loves you."

"I don't get your shirt," I said.

He looked down like he had forgotten what he was wearing.

"Me neither. I just thought it looked Eastery."

Brady came out of the kitchen balancing a carton of eggs on the back of his hand. My mom freaked out.

"Hey—be careful with that! What are you—"

"Relax, honey," Dad said. "It's part of his act. Go on, Brady."

Brady began his little speech:

"Welcome to Easter dinner, everybody. And what is Easter without eggs? Be careful, they're very fragile. Or *are* they?"

I nudged Rusty under the table. "He's so dramatic," I whispered.

Brady continued: "You may think you can crush an egg in the palm of your hand, but you're wrong. The egg is stronger than your hand. No matter how hard you squeeze, the egg will remain in one piece. Do we have any volunteers?"

"I'll try first. My shirt is junk. I've got nothing to lose." Flip grabbed an egg out of the carton and placed it in his hand.

"So, I just wrap my fingers around it and squeeze as hard as I can?"

"Yes, that is correct," Brady said.

Flip did just that. I waited for the explosion. But it never came. The egg stayed in one piece.

"You're holding back," Bob Hansen said. "Let me try."

Bob grabbed an egg and tried the same thing. Nothing.

"That's ridiculous," he said.

"Bart, have you tried this already?" Mom asked.

"Oh, yeah. I can't do it."

Rob Peterson tried next. He couldn't break the egg either. "That's amazing."

"Do we have a female volunteer? Maybe the women are stronger." Brady knew which button to push with us.

"Yeah, hand it over, kid," Mom said. "I have strong hands."

She squeezed. Nothing.

"What have you done to these eggs?" she asked.

"Nothing. It's sheer science."

Both Rusty and I tried it next. I thought maybe a smaller hand would bust the egg. No luck.

"What about you, Fawn?" Brady tried handing her a brand-new egg out of the carton.

"No, thanks," she said.

"Aw, come on!" Flip said. "You're not going to disappoint a little kid now, are you? What if you're the only person on earth who can break an egg in your hand? Don't you think he deserves to know?"

Dirty looks flew across the table between Flip and Fawn until Fawn finally gave in.

"Okay, give me the egg."

Brady took the egg back out of the carton and checked it carefully for cracks before handing it to Fawn. She grabbed it and put it in her palm.

"Okay, so I just squeeze, right? You guys aren't in on some kind of practical joke, are you?"

"You mean practical *yolk*?" Flip laughed and slapped the table, and all the water glasses shook.

"Very funny. Ha-ha." Fawn looked down at the egg and squeezed.

Nothing happened.

"This just seems ridiculous," she said. "It's a fragile little egg." She squeezed harder. "Are you sure this one's not hard-boiled?"

"I promise it's not," Brady said.

"What if I just turned it a bit ..." Fawn repositioned the egg in her hand.

"Make sure you keep it in your—"

Fawn squeezed, and the egg exploded.

"Palm." Brady's warning came a second too late.

The explosion itself only took a second, but it was the funniest second ever.

Pieces of shell flew all different directions, like broken glass. The yolk stayed together in one big blob, and landed right in the middle of one of Fawn's yellow polka dots. The egg white splattered everywhere—kinda like spraying hairspray—and it covered Fawn's face, hair, and neck. It pooled and dripped off her eyelashes and down the two curls on the sides of her neck.

Everyone sat there stunned.

I wanted to laugh, but I waited to see what Fawn did first.

Even Flip stayed quiet for this one.

The round yolk started to slide from one polka dot to the next, down the middle of Fawn's dress. She looked down and was able to catch it before it fell in her lap. She held it up in her hand and smiled.

"I knew I could do it."

That's when everyone roared with laughter.

"And now," she said, "I would like to take a shower." She got up and made her way down the hallway to the bathroom.

"Dinner will be delayed a few minutes," Mom said, and she got up to follow Fawn.

"Anyone care for an egg appetizer?" Flip asked as he pointed to the gloppy mess Fawn had left on the table.

"She should have listened to me. I told her to keep it in her palm. She dug her nails in. Oh, the embarrassment …" Brady gathered up the remaining eggs and trudged back to the kitchen.

When Fawn came out of the bathroom, her hair was in a ponytail—just like we saw when we were at her house—and she was wearing some of my mom's sweats, a t-shirt, and some slippers. And for the rest of the night she was different. Good different. Relaxed. If I didn't know better, I would have thought she switched places with a twin or something. She laughed at Flip's jokes, smiled even when I used bad manners, and she ate a lot—which she never does—and commented on practically every bite.

"I can't remember when I've had a better meal," she said as she popped a big bite of chocolate cake in her mouth. "Thanks for inviting me." She washed the cake down with a huge gulp of sparkling apple cider. "Yum. Now I need to walk a mile or so." She patted her belly. "Glad these are stretch pants." This *had* to be Fawn's happy twin sister.

"Mom, can I help you with the dishes?" I didn't really want to, but my good feelings took over and that question just popped out of my mouth.

"Absolutely not. I've got this covered. Why don't you all go out to the living room and get out some board games or something. I'll just clear these and take care of them later."

What a relief. I'd rather play games than wash dishes any day.

We all made our way out to the living room, where we saw Brady—kneeling backward on our couch and staring out the front window.

"Brady, whatcha doin over there?" I hoped he wasn't pouting over Fawn and the egg. He usually doesn't like when things don't turn out the way he planned.

"I'm not Brady, I'm Sam Shady—Private Eye. I'm on a case. Don't bug me."

We all looked at each other and shrugged. Flip couldn't stay out of it, though. He jumped on the couch next to Brady and looked out.

"I wanna play. Who are we spying on?"

Brady pointed out to the hedge that leads up to our front door.

"That guy."

That's when we all ran over to the window. A guy—outside?

Mom came in and wanted to know why we were all staring out the window.

That's when we saw him—a figure in a grey hooded sweatshirt ran down our driveway, jumped into a silver car, and drove off.

"Brady!" Mom pulled out her phone. "How long was he there?"

"I don't know. A little while. He kept looking in the window by the front door and then hiding behind the hedge."

"Why didn't you say something?" Flip asked.

"I'm a *private* eye. We keep things to ourselves."

"That's dumb," I said.

Mom called her station in Clovis, which is just a few miles from where we live in Fresno. "Hi, Jack—yeah, can you send a unit over to my house? We've had an intruder. No, not inside—just lurking by the front door. Thanks."

Brady looked like he was going to cry. "I didn't do anything wrong. He didn't look like a bad guy. I thought he was going to ring the doorbell ..."

"It's okay, honey. He probably just had the wrong address or something. Why don't you go upstairs and get a game for us to play?"

"I'll get Clue," he said. Then he ran upstairs like nothing had happened. Sometimes it's cool to be Brady.

The rest of us stood around, not sure what to do.

"A squad car will be here in a few minutes," Mom said. "I'll ask them to stay parked outside for the rest of the night." Then she turned to Fawn. "I've seen that car before—in front of your house. So who could be following you?"

Fawn sat down on the couch and grabbed a pillow.

"I'm the most boring person on earth. I can't think of anyone. Maybe they're following you. You're the cop."

Flip and I glanced at each other. I wanted to say it out loud but I didn't.

That's the same car that was in the parking lot at the Swiftriver office.

Maybe they're following Flip. Or ... me.

A chill ran through my whole body.

Chapter 31

I didn't sleep much that night. And when I did, I dreamed that a big, scary silver dog was chasing me. "Grrrrr, Grrrrrrrrrrrrr!"

I ran as fast as I could in my orange running shoes.

The dog got closer and closer. Then Sean appeared with a chocolate donut.

"Get away from me—he's going to catch me!" I shoved Sean aside and ran through Woodward Park. But now I had on my flip-flops and couldn't run fast. The dog caught me by the pants, I screamed—and then he dragged me down. I fell ... and slid into home plate.

"Safe!" The umpire yelled. TJ was cheering me on— wearing Rusty's Teal and Steal shoes.

Then I woke up. I ran to the window and looked out to see the police car still sitting at our curb. My heart was beating really fast, and I wondered if I had screamed for real or just in the dream. I expected my Dad to come in any second. Instead, Brady came into my room.

"What are you doing up?" I asked.

"Are they following you?"

"Who?"

"The guy out front. 'Cause you're famous."

"I'm not famous."

"Yes, you are."

"No, I'm NOT."

"Then how come someone's following you?"

"What? You don't make any sense! Anyway, the police are out there now. We're all safe."

He walked out.

At least in the dream I was safe.

Chapter 32

The next few weeks felt normal for the first time since the whole shoe girl thing started. I didn't have any photo shoots, so I actually played in a couple of softball games. We won both of them, which made TJ very happy. I got to hang out at TJ's house a few times, and she even invited Rusty over for one of our brownie-making sessions.

Rusty's dad started his job at Swiftriver, and he finally got paid, so Rusty got some new clothes.

"Just in time, I'm growing ... again," she said. I think Rusty's a whole head taller than me and TJ now. She's strong too, which is why she's our cleanup hitter. (That's the person who bats fourth in the lineup—the best batter on the team.)

Fawn even seemed to stay normal. (I call her "Easter Fawn.") She invited me over to her house to work out a few times.

"You need to increase your upper body strength for the Half Dome cables," she said.

When I couldn't even do one pull-up on her bar, she shook her head. "It's no use. Looks like we'll have to push you up."

"How high is it?"

"About eight thousand feet."

"Can't we take the jet?"

"Ha-ha. No."

Fawn got on the treadmill and turned it up as steep as it could go.

"You've got to get your legs ready. Hiking uphill is a lot different than running softball bases."

I watched her go for about five minutes. She sweated a lot, but she seemed like she could climb forever.

"How come you're in such good shape?"

"I'm not really."

"Huh. Yeah you are. You must like to work out."

She stopped the treadmill. "Here, get on. I'll go get us some sport drinks."

She turned it back to the steepest setting. "I wanna see a big sweat mark on your shirt by the time I get back."

"I don't remember seeing 'killer workouts' mentioned in the shoe contract."

I changed the setting to easy as soon as she left the room. There was no sweat mark when she returned.

"I guess you don't need this drink then." She chugged down my drink.

I guess Fawn was my "personal trainer" now. I wished she would pick a job and stick with it.

During those weeks, I kept having the dog dream. Sometimes it changed a little. The places and people in the dream were different, and the shoes I was wearing changed. But I always slid safely into home plate.

Maybe that's because Mom had arranged for a police unit to follow Fawn, so I felt safe when she was around. I hadn't figured out how to tell Mom that maybe the guy had been following me, since then I would have to tell her about the whole Flip thing, and I didn't want to get grounded. But considering what happened next, grounding would have been a good thing.

Chapter 33

"Mom, can you find missing people?"

I like to ask my mom questions like that when she's slightly distracted. In this case, she was getting my Half Dome supplies together on the living room table.

"What do you mean by missing? Like the kids on the milk cartons?" She kinda frowned.

"No—not that. I guess I mean people who might be hiding from someone. Would you be able to find them with all your police help?"

Mom went to the pantry and pulled out some energy bars.

"It depends on the situation. If they changed their name and their social security number, it could take some time. It also depends on where whey went. If they went to another country, it could be impossible. Why do you want to know?"

I wanted to know for Rusty, but I couldn't say that.

"I'm thinking of running away so I don't have to be a shoe girl anymore."

"What? Don't you even talk like that. Moms can always find their daughters."

But can daughters always find their mothers?

The supplies I needed for the Half Dome hike made me nervous: rain poncho (it might rain?), moleskin (some weird stuff for blisters and chafing—great), flashlight (we were starting the hike at 6:45 in the morning. Did they think we'd get home after dark?), lots of food (What? No snack bar on the way?), work gloves...

"Why do I need gloves?"

Dad came in from the garage carrying his daypack.

"For the cables. You'll have one on each side of you as you climb up the mountain, They're metal, and they'll bite into your hands if you don't have gloves."

"That sounds so fun," I joked. "I just ... can't ... wait."

"You arranged for that guide, right, honey?" Mom asked.

"Yes, Matt Rainier—from our church. Best in the business. He's been taking people on these kinds of hikes for years." There they went, talking like I wasn't there again.

"What do we need a guide for?"

"Your mom wants to make sure we come back in one piece. Matt knows what to look out for, so I hired him to come along. He's also a medic and a skilled rock climber."

"Does Bob know about that?" I asked.

"Oh, yeah. He's very supportive of the whole thing. He wants to protect his employees too."

As far as I knew, the only people coming on the hike were me, Dad, Flip, Fawn, and some reporter from *Outdoor Teen Magazine*. So now we had this Matt guy too. I was glad Fawn was coming so I wouldn't be the only girl. "Well, I wish Bob never planned this trip. I think *he* should have to go. It sounds too hard."

"But it won't be as long as you're wearing ... Riley Mae Rock Shockers from Swiftriver!" Dad held up the hikers like he was doing a commercial.

I grabbed one out of his hand. "The person who names these shoes is pretty creative."

Dad grinned from ear to ear.

"What? Tell me it's not you."

"Yeah, it's me. I am an advertising guy after all. And since I know this Riley Mae girl personally, they thought it would be a good idea for me to name each pair of shoes."

"How come you never told me that before?"

"Just in case you didn't like the names—didn't want you complaining."

Mom was still stuffing things in my pack. "Okay—I hope that's everything, because there's no more room."

Chapter 33

"I want to take my phone so I can text TJ when I'm at the top."

"You won't get service up there," Dad said.

I shoved my phone in a side pocket. "I have faith."

Chapter 34

The next morning started really early. We had to wake up at four o'clock to get ready and drive to the trailhead at Happy Isles in Yosemite National Park. I texted TJ.

Git up! I'm up!

She didn't text back.

I was actually more nervous than tired. School had let out for the summer just a week before, so I'd been getting lots of sleep on purpose. Fawn had scared me into being rested and ready for this hike.

At the trailhead we met up with our guide, Matt Rainier. He was friendly and funny as he described some of what we were going to experience:

"Pain, hunger, thirst. But mostly, awe."

We also met Nate Johnson, the reporter from *Outdoor Teen Magazine*. "We're a new publication—started with the goal of inspiring young people to get outside and discover natural beauty instead of always watching it on TV. This story will be in our first issue, scheduled to come out in July."

I guess the idea was for them to interview me throughout the hike so kids my age would know what to expect and want to do it too. Flip, of course, was going to take the pictures. In exchange for the story, the magazine offered to give Swiftriver free advertising in their magazine. Sounded good to me—except the hiking part.

Fawn looked happy and really sporty. She was wearing the Riley Mae Rock Shockers too. Mine had grey mountains on them with a red and pink background. Hers were the same, but the background was blue and green. The rest of her outfit was color coordinated with the shoes, and she had a grey ball cap on with her ponytail coming out the back. This was definitely "Easter Fawn."

"Did you eat breakfast?" She asked. "I hope not donuts, 'cause junk's not going to get you up this mountain."

"I know that. I ate cereal and turkey sausage, and I drank some orange juice."

"You wanna know what I ate?" Flip asked.

"No. I'm not in the mood to have my stomach turned right now," Fawn said.

"Okay, troops, it's time. Let's fasten up your packs and get going." Matt double-checked to make sure everyone had a properly balanced pack, and then he led the way up the first part of the hike—the trail to the Vernal Falls bridge.

After five minutes, I wanted to stop. The trail was steep, and I was huffing and puffing so much that my head was pounding. My stomach got all crampy too—and that made me nervous since Matt told us there were only three real bathrooms on the trail. If we had to go anywhere else, we'd have to find a bush.

"Can we stop a minute?" Dad's comment from the back of the group was a relief to me.

"Sure," Matt said. "Everything okay?"

"My head is throbbing." Dad took off his hat and sat down on a rock.

"That's normal. It's a pretty steep road to start out on. Your body just needs to get used to it." Matt went over to Dad and offered him a little packet of something.

"Try some goo. It'll give you a jumpstart."

Dad squeezed whatever the "goo" was in his mouth, and then rinsed it down with his water. "Okay, I'm ready."

My head felt better. I checked my watch. We'd been at this for ten minutes. Nate was looking at me and taking notes.

"Whatcha writing over there?" I asked.

"I'm writing that you look fresh and ready to go, but you have to wait for the lagging grown-ups."

"Oh." If he only knew how I really felt. "It's the shoes." I pointed to my Rock Shockers.

"Yeah, that's what you get paid to say."

Chapter 35

"Dad, how much money do I make doing this?" I figured this was a long hike, so I had time to ask a few questions.

Dad looked around. Nate had moved up to the front so he could interview Matt, and Flip and Fawn were behind us chatting and taking pictures.

Dad lowered his voice. "That's not really something we should be discussing here, honey."

"Well, is it enough to get rich?"

"Do you want to be rich?"

I thought about Rusty with no food in her house. Then I thought about TJ with the two hundred dollar bills in her pocket from her grandma. I remembered Flip's two hundred sponsored kids. It didn't make sense to me that some people have so much and others don't have anything.

"Yeah, I'd like to be rich. There's a lot I could do with a bunch of money."

"Well, sorry to tell you, but you're not going to get rich."

"Oh well."

"But you will earn enough to pay for four years of college."

"That's good, right?

Dad smiled. "Yep. Very good."

"I'm glad I'm doing it, then."

Just as I said that, we arrived at the Vernal Falls bridge.

Matt gathered us all together, and Flip took a picture. He had to protect his camera from all the mist that was blasting off the rocks from the huge waterfall.

"Hurry up," I yelled. "I'm getting soaked!" After Flip clicked another picture of the group, I ran off the bridge to a dry spot next to a tree.

"Anyone have a towel?" I asked.

Matt laughed. "No need to dry off. We haven't even hit the real wet part yet."

"What?" I looked up at the waterfall and wondered which direction we would go from here.

Matt must have read my mind, because he pointed up. "We're climbing up the side of *that*, and when we're done, we'll be up at the top right edge—where you see the water coming over."

I panicked and looked for a place to escape. And there it was—a little brown building.

"First bathroom stop, folks," Matt said.

I would have liked to stay in the bathroom, but it stunk too bad, so I got out quickly.

"So, Riley, how do you like the hike so far?" Nate had his little notepad out.

"It's great. So pretty. Can't wait to climb up to the top of the waterfall. I'm sure my Rock Shockers will help me run right up there."

"Running won't work for this leg of the journey," Matt said. "We're going to be on some granite stairs, and they get kind of steep. The water will be coming hard right in your face so you really need to be careful with each step. Don't take your eyes off your feet."

Great. All of a sudden I wasn't glad I was doing this.

We all put on our rain jackets and headed up the side of the waterfall. Matt stayed behind the group this time so he could keep an eye on all of us.

"If you get tired, just stop for a few seconds and catch your breath. Move to the right, against the rocks so that other groups can pass you on the left." I was amazed that there were so many people on the trail—and so many without good shoes. Some were even wearing flip-flops!

"Now that's dumb," Flip said as he pointed to a group of flip-floppers.

"And that's saying something coming from you," Fawn added.

"Lots of people attempt this hike without proper preparation," Matt said. "They don't realize how long and treacherous it is. There are numerous injuries each year."

"Do people ever die?" I asked.

"Oh, yeah. People have died on this hike."

I stopped walking. "What? I'm not going, then."

Fawn pushed me from behind. "Keep going, girl. You'll be fine. The ones who die are the ones who do risky things—which won't be you."

"What kind of risky things?" I asked.

"You'll see some at the top of the waterfall," Matt said.

I started to wonder if I would make it to the top of the waterfall. Matt wasn't kidding when he said we would be going on some steep stairs. Some were so steep my legs barely reached to the next one. The tops of my legs burned so bad that I wanted to stop, but I couldn't because the water was slamming into my face. My left ear was so packed with water that I couldn't hear out of it.

Finally, there was a resting place. A little tunnel in the rock provided some shelter from the water. Unfortunately, quite a few other people wanted to rest there too.

The flip-flop group was there, but now they were on their way down.

"Good choice," Matt said. Then he warned them to be careful not to slip on the way down. But he said it this way: "Your choice of footwear is not going to afford you any traction."

We all stayed in the tunnel for a minute or two, then started back onto the trail. About ten seconds later, we heard a scream.

Chapter 36

We all looked down. I expected to see a flip-flopper bouncing down the rocks. But it wasn't any of them. The scream came from Fawn. Thankfully, she wasn't in the waterfall. But she was sitting down on a step, holding her right lower leg. And there was blood all over the place.

"Everyone, just stay where you are. I'll check her out." Matt jumped up a couple of steps. "You forgot to watch your feet," he said to Fawn.

"Yeah," Fawn shook her head, "The scenery kind of hypnotized me."

I guess when she missed the step, her shin slid down the granite. It tore about a three-inch piece of skin off.

"Wow—you almost scraped down to the bone." Matt wiped Fawn's wound with an antiseptic wipe. She barely flinched, but I shivered. Flip took a picture of Fawn's leg. Nate started scribbling notes. We were all still getting soaked.

"Should we go back?" I asked.

Matt took out some kind of ointment, applied it to Fawn's leg and then wrapped it up with some bandages. "We don't all need to go back. We're not too far into this—I could take Fawn back and then catch back up with you guys."

"No way!" Fawn jumped onto her feet. "You think I'm some kind of sissy girl? I can make it. I've had much worse."

If you had asked me a few months ago if Fawn was a sissy girl, I would have said, "Of course." I thought of those first days with the makeup bag, the high heels, and the white skirt on the baseball field. Where was that Fawn?

"Let's get going," she said. "I want to get to the top of this waterfall."

So we kept climbing, steeper and steeper, until we hit some switchbacks at the top. Someone had put up a metal fence guard for the last few steps. At least if I fell now I wouldn't land all the way at the bottom of the waterfall.

Chapter 37

There were dumb people doing risky things at the top of the waterfall just like Matt said. They were hanging over the fence—taking pictures—and some had even climbed over the fence and were wading in the water just a few feet above the drop off. I wondered if they could read the sign right next to them:

WARNING
Fatalities occur each year in Yosemite. To avoid serious injuries or death, stay out of water above waterfalls, watch your footing on rocks, and obey all warning signs.

Then I saw another sign:

WARNING
You are entering Bear Country.
Take proper precautions.

I decided then and there that I wanted to be a warning sign obeyer—and live.

"Matt?" I pointed to the sign. "How do we 'take proper precautions' in Bear Country?"

"Bears are not too big a deal out here. They're actually trying to stay away from people. But just to be safe, I have some pepper spray. If we were going to camp overnight, we'd have to lock our food up. They are attracted to the smell."

"You think they'll sniff out Fawn's bloody leg?" Flip asked. Fawn smacked him.

Matt laughed. "No, bears actually prefer berries and things like that. I really doubt we'll see a bear today. They have better things going on."

We hiked about a half-hour longer and then took a break at the bottom of Nevada Falls.

"Better get a little snack," Matt said. "It's going to get steep again."

I sat down with my dad to eat an energy bar and an apple. When I pulled them out of my bag, I saw my cell phone. I took it out to take a picture and send it to TJ and Mom. The picture turned out fine, but there was no service to send it.

"I guess we're all on our own now," I said.

Matt checked his phone too. "Believe it or not, sometimes people can get reception at the very top of Half Dome,"

"If we do, I'm calling for a pizza." Flip licked his lips.

Matt laughed. "That would be an expensive delivery."

"There's pizza in the valley when we get back down," Dad said. "I'll buy for whoever wants it." From that point on, I kept an image of a pizza in my brain. All I had to do was get to the pizza.

Pizza was on top of Nevada Falls. (Not really. But I did eat some crackers, cheese, and pepperoni.) The climb to the top seemed even steeper than the one to the top of Vernal Falls. But the higher we got, the prettier everything got. I was starting to experience the "awe" that Matt had talked about earlier in the morning.

"How much farther?" Dad asked as we all finished up our snacks and got ready for the next part of the hike.

"A lot," Matt said. "But this next part is flat for awhile."

My legs were glad to hear that.

I looked over at Fawn, who was changing her leg bandage. Her right Rock Shocker had changed to the color of greyish-green dirty blood.

"Guess you'll need a new pair after this." I pointed to her messed-up boot.

"Boots can be replaced. I'm wondering about my leg." She attached some tape to her bandage.

"How does it feel?"

"Terrible now. For awhile it was numb. I liked that better."

"Here," Matt said. He handed Fawn some pain medication. "Take a double dose. It won't hurt, and it'll keep the inflammation down."

"How's your head?" Matt asked my dad.

"A little achy. It's gotta be the altitude getting to me."

Matt checked my dad's pulse. "It's normal for what we're doing so far, but let me know if you start to feel worse."

"Dad, do we have to go all the way to the top?" I stayed behind the group with my dad for awhile.

"We don't *have* to do anything, honey. But we *get* to do this together, and I think that's pretty special, don't you?"

"Yeah, but I don't want anything bad to happen."

"Not to worry. At the end of today we'll have an amazing story to tell."

Nate came over to talk to me about the hike so far. "So, Riley, what is the one thing you would say a teen needs to do this hike successfully?"

"Two sets of legs would help."

Nate laughed and scribbled.

"And then they could wear *two* different styles of Riley Mae Rock Shockers at the same time," I said.

Fawn high-fived me. "Good answer. You're starting to sound like a real spokesgirl."

Chapter 38

The little Yosemite Valley was a flat part of the hike, but it still wasn't easy. The thick sand made it feel like trying to hike at the beach, and my feet got tired of churning their way through the trail.

"Anyone low on water?" Matt took a tube-shaped thing out of his backpack.

"Yeah, me," I said, and I ran over to the side of the rushing river next to our trail. I knelt down to get a handful of water to splash on my face and take a drink.

"Stop!" Matt yelled.

"What? I was just getting some water."

"You can't drink that water until you run it through the purifier." He pointed to the tube thing.

"But it looks clean."

"You never know up here. Sometimes there are bacteria in the water that can make you really sick. Better not take a chance."

"Is anything safe out here?"

Fawn laughed. "Life's not safe—don't you know that?" She pointed to her leg.

I was starting to figure that out, and I didn't like it at all.

While Matt filled up our water containers, Nate sat down and asked me all kinds of personal questions— like what I like to do in my spare time, how well I do at school, who my friends are, and how I like working for Swiftriver. My dad was sitting right next to me, so I felt okay giving him the answers. I remembered back to that reporter from Arizona where I guess I said too much. I never told my parents about that.

"Okay, this is the last official bathroom for a long time, so don't ignore it." Matt pointed to a building in the Little Yosemite Campground.

I didn't have to go. "What do I do if I have to go in an hour?"

"Get behind a tree and dig a hole," Dad said.

Only a half-hour later, I had to go—really bad. Problem was, there weren't any really wide bushes or trees near the trail. Even though we were far into the hike, there were still a lot of people around, and I didn't want them watching me.

"Where should I go?" I asked Fawn. I thought I'd get some advice from her—not only about where to go, but how.

Fawn looked around. She pointed to a cluster of bushes that seemed like a long way away. "Go in there— see that tree in the middle of the bushes? Dig a hole at the base of it, squat over it, and lean your back against the tree for support."

"That way no bears can sneak up on you," Flip said. I didn't realize *he* had snuck up behind me.

"Where's the pepper spray when you need it?" Fawn said. She took off Flip's ball cap and slapped him with it.

"I don't know. What if there *is* a bear in there?" I asked.

Fawn slapped Flip again. "You see what you did? She's scared now."

My bladder couldn't take it any longer, so it didn't matter whether I was scared or not. I had to go.

"I'll get everyone to stop and wait for a few minutes." Flip ran up to the front of the pack where Matt and Nate and my Dad were.

I ran off to the bush cluster and then looked around to see if I could see people. Yep. I still could. So I moved over to another cluster that looked a little more private. As I got my hole ready, I heard some people laughing, so I ditched that place and went farther into the forest. Just when I thought I was going to have an accident, I finally found a private spot, right behind a really wide rock. I tried to go really fast, since I was scared to think of what would happen if a fox or a squirrel or a bird attacked me while I was busy. The whole situation made me appreciate the safe little bathroom I have at home. I decided I wouldn't even complain about having to clean it anymore.

After I filled up my hole with dirt, I got out my phone—just in case I had service. I thought it would be fun to text TJ and tell her that I had just peed in the woods and find out how things were going back at home. It felt like I'd been gone forever.

Rats, no service.

I tucked my phone back in my backpack and started back to the trail.

At least I tried to.

I looked back at where my little rock bathroom was, but then I got a little confused about which direction I came from to get there. Somehow, that second bush cluster had moved.

Wasn't it . . . that way? I turned around and looked for a path, but there wasn't one. Great. That's what I get for hurrying. Now I wished I had paid more attention to where I was going.

"Fawn?" I said, raising my voice a little. I didn't want all the people on the trail to think I was lost.

Where *were* those people now?

I couldn't hear anyone. Or see anyone. And all of a sudden, nothing looked familiar.

A cracking sound came from behind some trees. I

walked faster and tripped over a fallen tree branch and fell on the ground. Something skittered by right next to my head so I jumped back up and ran. I'm not sure which direction I ran in, though.

"Dad?" I raised my voice a little louder. Surely I would come out on the trail soon.

Get out your compass, Riley.

I obeyed the little voice inside and took out the compass Mom had packed.

I watched as the little pointy thing wound around to show north.

Yep, that's north.

But I had no idea how that was going to help me, since I didn't know which way I had come from.

I looked up hoping to see Half Dome. At least I could head in the direction of that.

But all I saw was trees and rocks.

Yikes.

My heart started to pound.

"Dad!" This time I yelled.

Check your phone again.

No service.

I stood there, looked up, and started crying.

Chapter 39

I had only been lost one other time before. At the zoo. I was creeped out by all the crawly things in the snake house, so I went to wait for my family outside. The problem was that I went out the *entrance* door, and they looked for me outside the *exit* door. My mom had zoo security on the problem in seconds, and I was found pretty much before I even knew I was lost. I got grounded for that.

But this was different. There was no security coming after me, and I didn't know how far I had gone off the path, so it could be awhile before I was found. If ever.

How am I going to survive out here by myself?

What if a bear comes?

How long till it gets dark?

The tears streamed down my face, and I couldn't breathe.

Fawn said life isn't safe. I wished she was wrong.

Chapter 39

"God, help me." Those were the only words I could think of to pray.

Blow your whistle.

Chapter 40

The whistle! It was clipped on the zipper-pull of my backpack. Matt had given it to me when we started the hike.

"If you get lost, blow this as hard as you can."

"I'm not getting lost," I had said. What a dummy.

I put the whistle to my lips, took a big breath, and then stopped.

I didn't want to look dumb. Especially in front of Nate, who would write about this in his magazine.

I looked around some more and still didn't see anyone.

Better dumb than dead.

I put the whistle to my lips again, took another deep breath...

And a loud, high-pitched squeal reached my ears.

But not from *my* whistle. (Well, I thought it was at first, because of the timing of the sound. But then I realized that I hadn't blown out, so it wasn't me.)

Chapter 40

I heard the squeal again, coming from a long way behind me. I turned and followed the sound.

"Riley!" That was Dad.

Thanks, God.

"Riley!" That was Fawn.

Okay, so I wasn't going to be dead. Now the only problem was how not to appear dumb.

I dried my eyes and put on a big smile.

This would have to be a great acting job.

Chapter 41

"Hey guys, what's goin' on?" I kicked a rock off the trail. La, la, la…

Dad ran over and gave me a big hug. "Are you okay, honey? You've been gone a long time. We thought you were lost."

I tilted my head a little. "I'm fine. Sorry I took so long."

"Why did you go so far? I showed you those bushes." Fawn looked like she'd been crying.

"There were people. I needed more privacy."

"I could have gone with you," she said. "Buddy system—remember?"

"Potty and buddy doesn't go together."

"It does if you don't want to get lost."

"I wasn't lost."

"Whatever you say, missy." She huffed off.

"Okay, well, we're glad you're here now." Matt hooked his whistle back on his pack. "I hope you don't forget to use your whistle if you *do* get lost. Sometimes people panic and run deeper into the woods."

I think Matt knew the real story.

"Don't worry about me. I'm not a panicky person."

I saw Nate scribble more notes.

"That's good, because the next part of the hike is not for the panicky." Matt gathered us all together to explain. "We're about to climb up the back of the Sub Dome—about eight-hundred granite steps."

"Ouch," I said.

"Yeah, especially if you fall. Because there's nowhere to go but straight down—four thousand feet."

Dad gave me a stern look. "That means you need to concentrate."

"No prob."

Dad grabbed me by the shoulders and stared me down. "No—concentration *is* a problem for you. You're always getting distracted. You *can't* get distracted any time during the next couple of hours. You got that?"

"O-kaaay, but what about Flip?"

"What *about* me?" Flip asked.

"You're worse than me at getting distracted."

"Okay, let's make a pact. We have to ignore the squirrels, no matter how cute they are." Flip and I had been giving the squirrels cuteness ratings all during the hike. He liked the ones that were chubby and funny, and I liked the ones that were slim and bouncy. All of them were super cute, and none of them were shy. I really wanted to feed them, but Matt said no.

"What squirrels?" I said.

"See? We got this." Flip gave a thumbs-up sign.

Dad didn't look convinced.

"You might want to reapply your sunscreen," Matt said. "There aren't going to be many more trees on the trail to shade you."

Gulp. Reapply? I sort of forgot to "apply" in the first place. No need to say anything to Dad about that. I got out my bottle and spread the gloppy stuff really thick over my dried-out shoulders and arms.

"Need some help with that?" Fawn grabbed the sunscreen out of my hand and started slapping a bunch on the back of my neck.

"Ow."

"Did you forget this earlier? You're getting pink back here."

"I knew I should have left my hair down."

"You should have put on sunscreen."

"I know. I forgot. Please don't tell my dad."

"I won't—*if* you admit to me that you were lost earlier."

"I wasn't."

"Mr. Hart? Can you come over here?" Aargh. Fawn is like a really annoying big sister sometimes.

"Okay," I whispered. "I was lost. And I freaked out, and I was about to blow my whistle. Are you happy now?"

"What's up, Fawn?" Dad had his fingers pushed into his neck as he walked over to us.

"I was wondering if you have any trail mix. Riley and I are craving some chocolate." She winked at me.

"Sure, I have some left." He reached into his pack and pulled out a bag.

"Why are you taking your pulse again?" I asked. "Are you feeling okay?"

"Yeah, I'm good. Matt just wants to monitor me since I'm the old guy of the group."

"Everyone ready?" Matt strapped his pack back on.

"Hey, do you guys mind if I pray for our group before we continue?" Dad's good at remembering important stuff like that.

"Yeah, me and Riley really need the help." Flip laughed.

Nate started scribbling again.

Dad prayed for safety, and then he thanked God for healthy bodies to climb and for the beautiful creation around us. As soon as he said "Amen," I asked everyone how old they were.

"Dad says he's the oldest—and I wanna know by how much."

I found out that Matt was thirty-two, Nate was thirty-one, Fawn was thirty (Flip had to tell me because Fawn refused), and Flip was twenty-seven.

"I guess you're too old to marry Breanne, then."

"Lucky for her," Fawn said.

"Hey, I'm not such a bad guy."

I tried to stick up for Flip. "I think you're fine. You even clean up nice—I saw a picture of you in a suit."

Flip stopped walking and looked at Fawn. Then he looked at me.

"Where did you see a picture like that?"

"At Fawn's house. In her hallway. There was some other guy in it too—from Swiftriver, I think."

He started walking again.

"Fawn, I didn't know you put pictures of me up in your house."

"Yeah, well I was desperate. Too much wall space and not enough art, so I had to settle for that picture of when we went to that wedding—"

"Mary and Smitty's wedding?"

"Yeah, Mary and Smitty."

"Was that the picture of us with Eric? I'm surprised you didn't crop me out of it."

"Well, like Riley said, you clean up okay."

"Who's Eric?" I asked.

"Just a guy that Fawn loves."

Chapter 42

I wanted to talk about Eric some more, but we got to the granite steps and my dad insisted that I stay near him. Climbing the steps was actually fun. There were a lot of them, and now I could see why my dad was so uptight about my paying attention. If you slip, it really is over. Nowhere to go but down—a long way. But it felt like I was on top of everything, and it was fun being up there. I just wish my dad could have relaxed a little. Just about every other step he said something.

"Watch out, Riley."

"Riley, watch your step."

"Honey, there's a bump."

"Be careful."

"Don't go too fast."

"Don't slip."

He was freaking me out. "Dad!"

"Sorry. I just don't want you to fall."

"I don't want to fall either."

It went on like that until we reached the top of the Sub Dome. Whew! What a relief. And then we all saw it. Half Dome.

I gasped. "We're going up there?"

Matt nodded. "All the way up."

I pointed to the side of Half Dome. "What is that thing that looks like an ant trail?"

"Those are people on the cables," Matt said. "And soon, we're going to *be* them."

"Whoa."

"How does everyone feel? It might be a good time for a light energy snack before we go up." Matt reached into his pack. "Goo, anyone?"

Fawn's bandage had turned mostly red from blood.

"I think I need a minute to change this." She sat down and began to unwrap her leg.

"It's amazing you can climb with that gross leg." I sat down and held the medical tape for her.

"You're always tougher than you think," Fawn said.

"You said you've had worse. What could be worse than scraping half your leg off?"

"Let's see ... broken collarbone, dislocated finger, broken leg, concussion ..."

"Did you fall off your high heels or what?"

"Huh?"

"Well, you don't seem the type to do physical stuff. At least you didn't seem like that type when I first met you."

Fawn finished taping up her leg and looked like she was thinking about something else for a minute. I waited for her to answer me, but she just got up and walked away.

So, I just sat there, annoyed that I couldn't figure Fawn out. I grabbed an orange out of my pack. Then I found out it was really a tangerine. That was great—I like tangerines much better. Sometimes things aren't as they seem. That's how it was turning out to be with Fawn. But in a good way.

Chapter 43

O kay, troops, it's time to get up there." Matt led us onto the "saddle"—a narrow part of the mountain that leads from the Sub Dome to the base of the cable trail. On either side of the saddle is ... a long way down.

"Put on your gloves, grab those cables, and don't let go no matter what," Matt said. "If you feel like you need to stop and catch your breath, rest on one of those wood planks that are attached to the rock. If you stop in the middle, your feet will just slip."

While everyone got out their gloves, Matt took me aside. He pulled some stretchy ropes and clips out of his pack.

"We're going to put you in a harness and attach you to the cables with these tethers and carabiners."

"Why? I can hold on fine."

"I know. But I don't want your dad having a heart attack. This is more about him than you right now."

I didn't want my dad to have a heart attack either, so I cooperated.

I actually had two carabiners (the clips) attached to me, so that every time I came to a pole, I could unclip and move one over while the other still held me in place. I felt like one of those kids who gets put on a leash at Disneyland so they don't get lost.

We had to go in a single-file line, since there were people coming down at the same time. It felt a lot like a Disneyland line, actually, except for instead of ropes on both sides guiding us through, we had metal cables. And at Disneyland, you don't *have* to hold the ropes or climb up a forty-five degree angle. (And at Disneyland, there's a fun ride at the end of the line.)

Fawn went first, then Flip. After Flip was Nate, Dad, me, then Matt.

"I'll catch anyone who falls," Matt said.

Just then, my empty water bottle popped out of the side netting of my backpack and bounced on the rock once ... twice ... and then disappeared over the ledge.

"You didn't catch that," I said.

I looked up and saw Fawn way ahead of the rest of us, climbing like a monkey, even with that messed-up leg. Show off.

Dad stopped on one of the wood planks. "I'm gonna rest a minute."

That was fine with me. My arms felt like they were burning off.

"You okay, Mr. Hart?" Matt was right behind me, with his feet sliding a little on the slick granite.

"Just out of breath."

"That's normal. Take as much time as you need."

I wasn't out of breath. Just out of muscle.

A couple of young men passed us on the right— outside of the cables. They were just crawling up the mountain.

I looked back at Matt. "Are they allowed to do that?"

"No rules out here. Except the rule of gravity. I hope it doesn't catch up with them today."

I pulled on my tethers and was thankful to have them.

After what seemed like fifteen minutes, Dad finally began to climb again. I couldn't see Fawn anymore. Flip and Nate had stayed back with us to take pictures and notes.

Flip leaned back to look up the mountain. "I bet she's already up there, eating her lunch on the diving board."

"Diving board? What's that?" I asked.

"A place you're not allowed to go near," Dad said.

Flip started climbing faster. "Hurry up, and you'll see."

Dad and I couldn't hurry up. It took us over an hour to get up the cables. Everything burned on me—my arms, legs, and lungs. And now my skin was beginning to show the burn too.

When I got to the top, I could barely squeak out a "Ta-da."

Dad looked like a zombie.

Fawn came over to welcome us to the top.

"Where you guys been? I've already had lunch and a nap. Made a lot of new friends too." Then she frowned. "Mr. Hart, you look as grey as this rock! You should sit down a minute."

Dad did, and he put his head down between his legs.

"I thought I was going to pass out a couple of times there." He shivered. "Anyone else cold?"

Cold? Was he kidding? I was sweating like a pig.

Matt pulled out a silver sheet from his pack.

"Here, put this emergency blanket on. It'll warm you up. You're suffering from mild altitude sickness." He dug in Dad's pack for an energy drink and handed it to him.

"I don't think I can drink this right now. I feel like throwing up."

"Chance it. You need the carbs."

Dad just sat there looking confused. Finally, Flip grabbed the bottle and opened it for him.

"Thanks, Flip."

"No problem. If you need to puke, try doing it over that ledge over there. No mess that way."

My dad managed a little laugh, so I knew he wasn't dying. I was a little nervous about how he was going to get down, though.

"Riley, let's go take some shots of you doing a handstand on the diving board," Flip winked at me.

Dad jumped up. "Over my dead body."

I noticed some color returning to his face.

"Okay, then how about if she just sits on the diving board? That's not even half as dangerous as what she's already done."

Dad couldn't argue with that. "Okay, but I'm coming with you."

"Great," Flip said.

I found out that the diving board is a pile of huge rocks that sort of hangs out over the top of Half Dome. I could see why my dad didn't want me out there. I crawled out not even halfway.

"Okay, that's as far as you go," Dad said. "Stay seated."

"Aw, Mr. Hart, I wanted her to lie on her stomach and hang over the edge so I can photograph the bottom of her shoes."

Even though I didn't do that, we did get some awesome shots on top of Half Dome. It was so much bigger up there than I thought. I looked around to try to figure out just how big. Hard to tell when all you can see is rock and sky. And, all of a sudden, clouds.

"What time is it?" I asked Matt. "It's getting dark around here."

"Time to get down, I'm afraid. Looks like some afternoon thunderclouds are starting to move in. Those weren't in the forecast, but it's always a possibility up here."

I didn't want to get down. It took too much work to get up. "Can't we just stay up here a little longer?"

"Not unless you want to get hit by lightning," Matt said.

I heard a little rumbling in the distance. Where had those clouds come from?

"Okay, but I want to send Mom and TJ a picture first." I pulled out my phone to check if I had service. Nope. But it had nothing to do with the signal. My battery was dead.

"Rats! Why did I leave my phone on all that time?"

"Here. Try mine." Dad handed me his phone. His had battery and a signal, but a very weak one. He also had a text message from Mom.

I took a picture of Dad with practically nothing but sky in the background. Then I went over close to a ledge and took a picture of part of Yosemite Valley—four thousand feet down.

I tried to send the picture messages, but they kept failing.

"Such a weak signal up here," Matt said. "Usually only texts work."

So I decided to try that. But first I took a peek at Mom's message:

Prints came back.

F&F not who they say they are.

Lives may be in danger.

What? I felt a rush of adrenaline shoot through my body. What was this text about? Whose lives? And who are F&F? What prints?

"Dad? I think you should look at this."

Dad said something back, but his voice was drowned out by another thunder rumble. He grabbed the phone from me and pushed me toward the cables.

Now Matt was barking orders. "Get down as quickly and safely as you can. Those clouds are still a ways off, but they move fast."

Nate was the first one on the cables. "Do I go down backward or forward?"

"Either way," Matt said. "I prefer to see where I'm going."

Matt hooked me up and told me to face forward.

After Nate it was Matt, me, Dad, Flip, and Fawn.

Wait. Flip and Fawn. Could they be F&F?

"I wanna hang out a little longer and enjoy the view," Fawn said. She was kind of smirking too—and suddenly that made me nervous.

Lives in danger.

Whose lives? That was a stupid thought since we were all hanging off the side of a cliff. It's just that all of a sudden I didn't know whom I could trust. Except Dad.

"I think I see your water bottle graveyard down

there," Dad joked. I didn't laugh. Instead, I gripped the cables harder as I slid down the rock. That caused the rubber on my gloves to burn from the friction. It smelled really awful.

"My feet are slipping," Nate yelled from the front.

"You need a pair of Riley Mae Rock Shockers!" Flip yelled back.

Nate was too busy holding on to jot that down in his notebook.

"Hey, Riley, let's get a ton of pics on the way down from here." The next thing I knew, Flip was standing next to me—outside the cables.

I yelled. "Stupid! Get in here!" But then I wondered if I wanted Flip next to me at all.

"Hey—relax. I was holding on the whole time." Flip ducked under and got inside next to me.

I frowned and moved over to hold the other cable.

"You all right? You look scared. I thought you liked being up here."

"I just want to get down now. That's all."

Another rumble.

"That one was farther away. I think we're going to dodge a bullet." Matt was obviously talking about the lightning storm, but why did he have to mention bullets when I just read a text that said *lives in danger?*

"Okay, Riley," Flip said. "Stay calm now. I'm going outside for a minute—it'll get me in better position to take some pictures. You just smile and cooperate so I can do this quickly."

"Flip, don't be an idiot!" Fawn scolded him like a mom from up above.

"These pictures are gonna be great!" Flip took ten shots—I counted. If he took any more, I was going to scream.

"There. You see? Nothing to it."

"Okay, daredevil," Dad said, "Get back inside now."

Flip smiled and let go of the cable for a second to place his camera back in his shoulder bag.

And that's when the unthinkable happened.

Chapter 44

A big blue backpack fell from up above—right toward Flip and me. It hit Flip hard and knocked his feet out from under him.

I couldn't say or do anything. I felt like someone punched me in the stomach as I watched Flip go down, hit a bump, fly up, and then skid down again.

Oh God, please help him!

I saw him look up at us and grin—so I thought maybe he'd grabbed on to something, but then he yelled as he disappeared under the curve of the rock. From where we stood, we couldn't see if he had stayed on the path, or if he had fallen off the cliff.

Fawn screamed and came running down the cable trail.

"Move! Get out of my way!" She pushed through the people and flew—that's what it really looked like—down through the cables and under the curve, so we couldn't see her anymore either.

The rest of us were just frozen in place. I started to cry.

Next I heard Matt's voice. "We need to keep moving! Whatever's happened, we can't fix it from up here. Let's make sure we all get down safely, and then we'll deal with whatever we find. Just focus on listening to me and nothing else."

"Do what he says, Riley." Dad said.

Matt kept yelling out directions, like "Step forward, take a breath, watch your feet," and stuff like that.

"Almost there," he finally said. I had no idea how long we had been climbing down, but it seemed like only seconds.

Then I heard the sobbing. Fawn's sobbing. And I saw a large crowd looking over the side of the saddle.

Oh no. Flip's dead!

Matt unhooked my harness from the cables and then told me, Dad, and Nate to go sit down—away from the crowd. Matt ran over and started ordering the crowd to do things. I heard him tell some of them to go get a ranger (I don't know where from) and some to see if they had phone reception so they could call emergency services.

"You know what our job is—right?" Dad grabbed my hands and he started to pray. "Lord, we don't know where Flip is right now, but protect him and everyone else who is trying to help him. Please, don't let him die, Lord. Amen."

I buried my head in my hands. I didn't want to look anymore. Then my face got hot, so I pulled my hands away and just stared down ... at my shoes.

Those dumb things. If it hadn't been for them, we wouldn't be here. And we'd all be okay.

"I have to throw up," I said. I grabbed my stomach and got up to find a bush. There wasn't one. Just rocks. No matter—I didn't care who saw me. Dad followed and knelt down next to me to wipe my face with a damp cloth.

"I'm sorry, honey. This is my fault for allowing you to do this. I put all our lives in danger."

Lives in danger.

I grabbed Dad's shirt. "Where's your phone?"

He looked surprised. "In my pack. Why?"

"You have to read Mom's text. It said something about us being in danger. I think someone is trying to kill us!"

"What? Riley, calm down. You're not thinking straight."

I got up and ran to Dad's pack.

Matt came over to meet us. "Flip's alive. He landed right on the edge of the rock."

"Thank God!" Dad's eyes leaked tears and so did mine.

"He doesn't appear to have any broken bones, but he's unconscious and his pulse is very weak."

I wiped my tears on my sleeve and breathed a sigh of relief. "So, what's gonna happen now?"

"We've sent word to the rangers at Little Yosemite Valley, and we also sent a message up the cable trail for someone up there to call emergency services. We're not in phone range here."

Dad scratched his head and looked up at the sky. "How long till someone comes?"

"Hard to tell," Matt said. "I don't know if a helicopter can come up right now with storm clouds in the area."

"Then we'll just pray those clouds away," Dad said.

"We'd all appreciate that," Matt said as he went back to tend to Flip. I was grateful that Matt had some medical knowledge.

So we prayed again. This time, Dad took longer. I had a hard time concentrating, though, since I couldn't stop thinking about the text from Mom.

He finally said amen, and I pushed the phone in his hands.

He scratched his head as he read it.

"What prints is she talking about?" I asked. "Who's F&F?"

Dad thought for another moment. "Riley, you shouldn't have looked at this."

"I'm sorry! I wasn't trying to be nosey, but you have to tell me what it means!"

Dad put the phone back in his pack.

"No, I don't. It has nothing to do with this situation."

"Yes it does. I know it does!" I was yelling, and people started looking at us.

Dad grabbed me up in a big hug and then whispered in my ear. "Trust me, honey. We're all going to be fine. We'll talk more when we get home."

Chapter 45

I wasn't allowed to go over near where Flip was, but once in awhile the crowd cleared so I could see him a little. He was lying right on the edge of a cliff. No one was moving him, and that was making me nervous. I was afraid he would wake up and roll over the wrong way and fall all the way this time.

And why didn't he wake up?

Fawn paced around the crowd, looking up at the sky. How long would it take for the helicopter to get here? A ranger from Little Yosemite Valley arrived with a big pack with some medical gear. He put a splint on Flip's ankle and a board under his head. Then he threw one of those silver emergency blankets on him, like Dad had earlier.

Actually, my dad still didn't look so good, and from time to time I saw him grab his chest and try to catch his breath. Then he'd sit down and put his head between his legs.

"Dad, are you okay?"

"I'm not great, but I'm better off than Flip." Matt came over and took Dad's pulse again.

"When the helicopter gets here, I'm going to ask them to take you too. You're not any better, and getting to a lower altitude is pretty much your only cure right now. I don't want to chance losing you on the way down." Matt smiled as he walked off.

"Losing you?" I said to Dad.

"He's just kidding. But I think I will take that helicopter ride."

"If it ever gets here."

The thunderclouds were gone now. If the helicopter didn't make it up here soon, it would be dark—and cold.

I wanted to go talk to Fawn, but I had no idea what to say. Dad wouldn't let me go over there anyway.

Nate tried to go over and talk to her—but that didn't go well. Her arms flew all around and I heard her say, "Don't even think about reporting this in your magazine!"

Dad went over to say something to Fawn, but I couldn't hear a thing, because all of a sudden there was a loud rumbling sound. I strained to see where the sound was coming from, but all I saw was a never-ending sky.

Then I saw it—a helicopter rose up from below us and began to circle around the area where Flip was.

The ranger motioned for the crowd to move out of the way. Many of the people had already made their way back down the granite steps, and no more people were being allowed to go up the cables, so there weren't many of us left on the saddle of Half Dome. But there still wasn't much room, so we all moved to the sides so the helicopter could touch down. It actually flew over our heads and landed on Sub Dome, right behind us.

Fawn stayed at Flip's side until the rescuers asked her to move. They slid a bigger board under his body, and it looked like they taped him to it with duct tape. Then they put him in a basket and carried Flip to the helicopter.

Matt came over to where we were standing. "You guys hurry up and get over to the copter. It's going to take off in a minute!"

We grabbed our gear and jogged up the hill to the top of Sub Dome. Everyone had been cleared out of the way, and the spinning blades were throwing dust up all over the place.

Matt yelled at the guys in the helicopter. "These two have to go—he's suffering from altitude sickness, and she's his daughter."

The medical technician reached out his arm and grabbed us both up into the helicopter.

"Wait, I have to go too!" Fawn reached her hands up.

I saw the technician shake his head. "We're running

out of room. Only injured and family." He motioned for the pilot to take off.

Fawn shrieked. "You can't leave me! I'm his sister!"

Chapter 46

Next thing I knew, Fawn was in the helicopter. She was sobbing again and rubbing Flip's arm. I handed her a tissue from my pack. She wiped her face.

"Thanks, Riley." Then she looked up at me. "Are you doing okay? Some personal assistant I am."

"I'm fine … well, no, that's a lie. I'm sick to my stomach, and I hate that all this happened."

"Yeah, me too."

"But now I know why you guys fight."

"Huh?"

I smiled. "You and Flip. You fight because you're brother and sister. Just like me and Brady. Now it all makes sense."

"Oh."

"Riley, I don't think Fawn really wants to talk about that right now." Dad sat on a seat, wiping his face with a damp towel.

"No, it's okay, Mr. Hart. Yes, Flip's my brother, and we

do fight—but we're mostly kidding. I really love him a lot."

That made me think about my brother and how mean I am to him in a non-kidding way. All of a sudden I felt really bad.

One of the medics came over to hook an IV up to Flip.

"Gotta get him some fluids," he said. "What happened up there, anyway? This guy looks like he's in good enough shape to handle that hike."

Dad explained. "Someone up above us lost their backpack, and it hit him. He fell probably seventy-five feet. We don't know how he landed, but I'm glad he didn't go off the side."

"What happened to the person who lost the backpack? Did they fall too?"

We all looked at each other.

"Did you guys ever find the person who lost the backpack?" Fawn asked.

Dad sat up straighter. "No, I was so shocked at what was happening to Flip that I didn't even think to look for that person."

"Well, that just doesn't make sense," the medic said. "You'd think that if they fell too, someone would have seen something. And if someone just dropped a pack, they'd meet you all down at the bottom to find out if everyone was okay, or apologize, or something."

"Maybe they were too scared and just ran away," I said.

"That would be cowardly," Fawn said. "How could they live with themselves?"

The medic got up and looked out the window. "Looks like we'll be touching down in about five minutes. We'll have some paramedics meeting us out on the helipad with a gurney for our friend here. We'll need to clear him out, so just stay put until I tell you to move."

Chapter 47

I've never entered a hospital from the roof before. I've also never ridden in a helicopter before. As we landed, I realized that I had hardly paid attention to the ride at all.

A bunch of people were waiting for us on the roof. The paramedics were there with a gurney for Flip. Other hospital employees were there with two wheelchairs—one for Dad and one for Fawn. Bob Hansen was there—and so were my mom and Brady.

"Mom, what are you doing here?" I asked.

"Matt called from the ranger station."

"You're sooo lucky," Brady said. "I never got to ride in a helicopter."

I glared at my brother. "Don't be ridiculous. This was not a lucky day."

Fawn jumped out of her wheelchair to go hug Bob Hansen. She kinda flopped on him and started crying again.

"Danny's not waking up! He fell really far, and I think he hit his head!"

Who's Danny?

Bob Hansen guided Fawn back down into her wheelchair.

"Honey, let's not panic yet. Let's just be thankful you're here now so he can get the help he needs."

A guy wearing a suit asked us to keep moving. "Let's get you folks inside to our emergency department. Looks like you need some tending."

We went inside a little room with an elevator, but Mom, Brady, and I had to wait with the suit guy for the second trip since all the messed-up people in the wheel-chairs had to go first.

I wanted to ask Mom some questions about the text she sent Dad, but Brady and that guy were there so I just stayed quiet.

"Are you okay, honey?" Mom asked. "You didn't get any injuries, did you?"

I thought about how I got lost and about the backpack almost hitting me.

"No, I'm fine. Just tired."

"You poor thing. I'm so sorry today didn't go well." She hugged me.

That's when I lost it. And then I didn't care who was there.

I started crying so hard I could barely catch my

breath. My shoulders shook, and tears flew out of my eyes and bounced off my Rock Shockers.

"I saw your text! Who are F&F? Whose lives are in danger? Were you talking about us? Mom, I was so scared! And then Flip fell—"

"It's okay, Riley. There's nothing to worry about. I'm sorry you saw that message. That was about something else."

I sniffed. "Really?"

"Yes, really." Then she looked at the suit guy. "She must be in a little bit of shock."

He nodded. "We can check her in too. Maybe administer a sedative."

The elevator dinged and the doors opened.

"That won't be necessary," Mom said.

"Man, you freeeeeaked out," Brady shook his head and went to sit down in the emergency waiting room. I wanted to hit him. Then I thought about Flip and Fawn and decided not to.

Chapter 48

We waited for a long time in the emergency room lobby before Dad came out.

"I'm fine. They gave me some electrolytes and told me to take a couple days off and stay low. Have you heard anything about Flip?"

Mom shook her head. "Nothing. I don't even know where they are."

Dad shrugged. "Do you think we should take the kids home and wait for news there?"

"No. We need to stay here." I saw Mom look over her shoulder, so I looked over there too. A policeman was walking over to talk to Mom.

"I'll be right back," she said.

Dad looked at me and Brady. "Have either of you seen a candy machine around here?"

"Let's go find one!" Brady turned off his video game and started running down the hallway.

Dad grabbed my hand and pulled me out of my chair.

"C'mon. The main lobby will be more fun than this place."

I tried to eavesdrop when we passed Mom and the policeman, but Dad was pulling me too fast.

There was candy in the lobby. There were a couple more policemen too.

"Dad, why are there so many police around here?" I asked.

"It's a big hospital. Just security, I guess."

"Are we in Fresno?"

Brady smirked. "Duh."

I pointed up. "Excuuuse me, but I came from the sky. How am I supposed to know where I am?"

"Yeah, we're in Fresno, I think." Dad grinned and shook his head. "Not sure what hospital, though."

Brady scratched his head. "How come you don't know? You're the dad!"

"It's been a weird day, buddy."

"Well, I'm gonna find out." I walked over to the front desk of the lobby. "Where am I?" I asked the kind-looking, older lady at the desk.

She laughed a little. "Community Regional. Fresno, California."

"Thanks. I knew the California part. It's just that I flew in."

"Oh, that sounds exciting. Is everyone okay?"

"I hope so." I looked down at the floor and shivered a little.

"Would you like a blanket?" The woman got up and pulled a brand-new, fluffy pink blanket out of a cupboard behind the desk. "You can keep it."

It looked warm and cozy. "Sure."

She came around the desk, opened the blanket up and wrapped it around me—even covering my head like a hood. "That should make you feel better."

"It does. Thanks."

"You're welcome. Let me know if you need anything else."

"Okay."

I found a really comfortable couch right across from the nice lady's desk, and I plopped down and picked up a teen magazine to read. When I opened it up, there I was, in a shoe ad, running at Fresno State.

"Ugh." I put the magazine back, threw the blanket over my head, and closed my eyes. I felt like I could fall asleep. I actually started to drift off when I heard a man talking to the lady at the desk.

"Excuse me, ma'am? I'm looking for Flip Miller. I was told he was at this hospital."

"Let's see. Oh yes. He's in ICU. Fourth floor."

"Thanks."

So Flip was in ICU. That didn't sound good. I flashed back to the scene of him falling and my stomach cramped. I took the blanket off my head and watched as a man in a baseball cap and a blue sweatshirt headed toward the elevator.

The guy looked familiar, but I couldn't remember where I'd seen him. Before I could figure it out, the elevator doors opened and he was gone.

Bob Hansen and Fawn came out of another elevator. They were smiling.

I grabbed my blanket and ran over to where Dad and Brady were sitting.

"Flip's awake! And he's talking. He can't remember a thing about the fall. But he's awake!" Fawn picked me up and spun me around.

"Thank God," Dad said.

"Is he gonna be okay?" Brady asked. "I brought his camera." Brady held up the old camera Flip had given him. I don't know what that had to do with anything.

"He's got a pretty severe concussion and a broken ankle, and they're going to X-ray more body parts when he's feeling better," Bob said.

"Can I go see him?" Brady asked.

"No, honey, I'm afraid you're not old enough." Fawn said. "But you can go, Riley. He asked you to bring him some jerky."

"Luuuucky!" Brady smacked me on the arm.

I actually felt a little sorry for Brady. "How about if I go in and take a picture of him for you?"

He handed me the camera and smiled a little. "Well … okay." Huh, I expected him to whine.

"I guess we can all at least go up to the ICU waiting room. And maybe we can find your mom on the way." Dad helped us gather our things, and we took off toward the elevator.

"We'll meet you up there in a minute. We're going to grab a milkshake or something." Bob put his arm around Fawn, and they went to the cafeteria.

Chapter 49

We found Mom in the hallway outside the ICU waiting room. She was talking on the phone, and she waved us by as we passed her. (I've seen her do that tons of times. There's no use interrupting her.)

The ICU waiting room was nice and big, and a TV in the corner of the room was playing one of the Star Wars movies. Brady went right over to stare at it. I plunked down on a chair while Dad used the phone on the wall to see if we could go in to see Flip. Across the room from me were more chairs and that guy in the blue sweatshirt.

It was really starting to bug me that I couldn't figure him out. He kept looking from side to side, but he never looked right at me. I wanted him to notice me, 'cause maybe he would figure out who I was and say some-thing. So I tried to make a scene by flipping my blanket around and then by saying some of the Star Wars lines out loud. Finally, I got up to get a magazine at the table that was right next to him.

Dad finally hung up the phone. "Okay, Riley. We can go in, but we need to wait for Mom so she can watch Brady."

Brady looked up from the TV. "I don't need anyone to watch me."

"Yeah, you do," I said.

"No, I don't!"

"Yes, you do!" I guess I couldn't give up fighting with my brother just yet.

Brady looked around the room and pointed to the guy in the sweatshirt. "Okay, he can watch me." Then Brady's eyes got big.

"Hey ..." Brady said. He got up, walked over to me, and reached for my hand, which he never does. He led me over to Dad, who was sitting down waiting for Mom.

"Let me go, Brady. Your hand is slimy."

He wouldn't let me go. Then he started whispering something in my ear.

"What? You're slobbering, and I can't tell what you're saying. Spit in Dad's ear."

Mom came in then.

"Oh good, you're here," Dad said. "Riley and I are going in—"

"That's him!" Brady pointed at the sweatshirt guy.

The sweatshirt guy got up to leave.

"He's the Easter sneaker!"

Sweatshirt guy took off running.

Mom went after him.

We followed Mom. But Mom moves really fast. We barely got into the hallway when we heard Mom call for help from two policemen down at the end by the elevators. They ran toward the sweatshirt guy.

"Stop right there!" Mom yelled.

Sweatshirt guy ran past the first elevator toward the stairwell, but Mom had caught up by then, and she and the two policemen jumped on him and dragged him to the floor.

The policemen pulled the guy's hands behind his back and put handcuffs on him.

"I can explain! I haven't done anything wrong." His voice sounded familiar to me too. But from where?

The other elevator door opened, and out walked Bob Hansen and Fawn—practically right into the pile of people on the floor. There was a little scuffle, and most of Fawn's milkshake flopped out of her cup and onto her shirt.

"Oh, great." Fawn wiped her shirt with her hand and then looked down at the sweatshirt guy.

"What in the world—Eric? Is that you?"

"Sam!" He yelled.

"What are you doing?" Fawn looked shocked.

"He's getting arrested." Mom had the policemen pull the guy up off the floor.

"Sam, tell them I haven't done anything wrong."

"Look—Mrs. Hart—this is some kind of mistake."

"Fawn, this is the man who's been following you, and I'd be willing to bet he had something to do with Flip's accident."

"No! I can explain," Eric said.

"You can do that down at the station." Then the two policemen dragged him away, down the stairs.

All of us who were left in the hallway just stood there, shocked. Bob took Fawn's empty milkshake cup from her, placed it in a drink caddy on the floor, and smiled. "Sorry about your drink. You want my lemonade?"

And that's when I remembered.

Lemonade.

Arizona.

The news reporter.

Eric.

"Hey—who's Sam?" Brady asked.

Chapter 50

We didn't get to see Flip that day. Instead, Mom and Dad took us home while the "mess" got sorted out.

"I think he was talking to me—Sam Shady," Brady said in the car on the way home.

"What?" I shook my head and pulled my phone out of my backpack. Still dead. Oh well. How would I even begin to text all this to TJ?

"When I saw the Easter sneaker, I was Sam Shady, private eye. That's the only Sam I know."

Mom turned around in her seat. "You guys are not to talk to anyone about what happened today, you got that?"

So much for texting. Brady frowned, put on some earphones, and started playing a video game.

"Who is Sam, Mom?" I asked.

"I don't want to get into that now. We'll explain everything tomorrow. At least everything *you* need to know." Great. That wouldn't be much.

"Lynda, it's been a hard day. Can't you tell us something?" Dad looked like he needed to sleep for a week. "Were we really in danger up there on Half Dome?"

Mom sighed. "I hope not. But I'm pretty sure Flip and Fawn were."

"So the F&F in your text was Flip and Fawn?" I knew it.

"Well, yes. But their real names are Daniel and Samantha Stevens."

Dad rubbed his neck. "Drake Stevens' kids?"

"Yep."

"Who's that?" I asked.

"Drake Stevens was a very rich real estate developer in New York." Dad said.

"Was?"

"Yes. He was killed in a construction site accident a few years ago."

"Flip and Fawn's dad was killed? That's terrible!"

"I know," Mom said. "The worst part is that it wasn't an accident. Flip and Fawn—I mean, Daniel and Samantha—found evidence to prove that people in their own company plotted to kill their father."

"Did the people go to jail?" I asked.

"Yes—for a long time." Mom looked down and then at Dad.

"Good," I said. "But, I don't understand. Why are Flip and Fawn here in Fresno working for Swiftriver?"

Chapter 50

"They're hiding out." Mom turned around in her seat and looked at me. "And they don't just work for Swiftriver. They *are* Swiftriver."

Chapter 51

That night I dreamed about the silver dog again. Only this time it was a wiener dog, and he was wearing a gray hooded sweatshirt. Sean was there again, holding out a chocolate donut, saying "Here, Eric, come and get Flip!" Then I saw shoes—green-and-gray Rock Shockers, running down a granite mountain, and I heard my voice scream, "Jesus! I can't do this anymore!"

And I heard a woman's voice say, "You're always tougher than you think."

Then I woke up. The clock on my nightstand said it was 10:00 am. I've never slept that late in my life, and my stomach was growling. Thankfully, I smelled bacon downstairs.

Bacon wasn't the only thing waiting for me downstairs. There were also cinnamon rolls, Fawn, Bob, and that wiener dog—Eric.

I'm glad I was wearing my good pajamas.

"So, you're not a reporter, are you?" I asked.

He shook his head and took a bite of a hot cinnamon roll. "No. Sorry I misled you. I was trying to find my brother and sister."

"Who's that?"

Fawn spoke up. "Eric's my brother."

"I thought Flip was your brother."

"He is too. Flip and I have the same mom and dad. Our mom died when we were little, and then our dad married Eric's mom, and they had Eric. We lived in the same house for about ten years, and then our parents got divorced."

"Oh. That's kinda confusing." I grabbed a plate and a bunch of food. I took a huge bite of a cinnamon roll, and then thought about asking Eric why he had been sneaking around so much, but I had to chew on my thoughts for a minute, so the adults took over the conversation. I'm not sure where Brady was.

"So, how did you find out who we were?" Fawn asked my mom.

"I lifted your fingerprints off your water glasses at Easter. It took awhile to get the results back. You guys have done a good job covering your tracks."

"So, you suspected something was wrong?" Bob Hansen—if that was his real name—asked.

"My wife is suspicious of everyone," Dad said.

"It was the jet—and the fact that your company had

such a big factory and lots of employees after only being in business for a couple of years."

"We didn't want our money going to waste on just us. It's hard for the Stevens family to just sit around and do nothing." Fawn grinned. "So Flip let me choose what kind of company we should start."

"So you're the creative genius behind Swiftriver shoes?" Dad asked.

"I guess, but I just had the interest in sports and shoes. We needed a business expert we could trust, so we got Bob over here."

"You're not a brother too, are you?" I swallowed quickly so I could ask that question.

Bob laughed. "No, I was Flip and Fawn's business teacher in high school."

"Huh?"

Mom's phone rang, so she got up and went into the kitchen to talk.

Fawn continued. "Flip was a terrible business student. He always liked art and photography—stuff like that. He would have failed the class, but Bob tutored him during lunch every day."

"Think of what Dad would have done if Flip had failed business!" Eric slapped Bob on the knee.

"We weren't going to let that happen," Bob said. "I didn't need Drake Stevens breathing down my neck..."

Mom came out of the kitchen. "That was Matt. He

said some climbers found a blue backpack halfway down the mountain."

I had totally forgotten about Matt and Nate. I guess they had to hike back down the mountain after we flew away in the helicopter.

"Did they find any ID? I hope no one else fell." Fawn looked panicked all over again.

"Uh, no, I doubt it. They checked all the pockets. Didn't find a thing. But the center compartment was filled with rocks."

"Who would carry rocks all the way up Half Dome?" I asked.

Dad looked at me sternly. "I'm pretty sure no one carried them *up*."

Fawn stood up. "Are you saying that someone filled the backpack with rocks, and deliberately dropped it on Flip?"

"That's my guess," Mom said.

I stopped shoving food in my mouth for a minute. "Why would someone want to hurt Flip?"

"For revenge," Eric said. "After Flip and Fawn testified against the people who had our dad killed, lots of them went to prison. There might be a few people still around who are mad about that."

"And that's why you're hiding out?" I took a drink of orange juice. "Sounds like a bad movie."

"I wish it were," Fawn said.

"By the way, I like the name Samantha way better than Fawn."

"Me too," Fawn said. I noticed she was wearing blue jeans, a t-shirt, and running shoes.

"You don't really like high-heels and skirts and floppy hats, do you?"

Eric laughed. "Fawn? Liking to dress up? That'll be the day! Flip's the one who likes to dress up."

My mouth dropped open.

"Riley, your mouth is full of food!"

"Sorry, Mom. It's just … Flip? Dressing up? That's hilarious!"

"And that's not all." Fawn continued. "He buys all those 'foofy' clothes *for* me. I hate shopping."

Mom's phone rang again. This time she stayed in the room to talk.

After a couple of minutes talking to whomever it was, she told us that Flip had moved to a regular hospital room.

"They expect him to get out today."

"Get out? Of the hospital?" I couldn't believe it. I thought he was dead yesterday.

Fawn smiled. "Yeah. We went to see him this morning after I saw the doctor for my shin. All his X-rays and scans came back clear. He's got a cast on the ankle, and he has to take it real easy for a few days, but he's going to be just fine."

I thought about all that for a moment. That was a miracle. God had answered Dad's prayer up on the mountain.

"So what do we do next?" Eric asked.

Bob spoke up. "Maybe you guys need to get out of Fresno for awhile."

"What do you mean by 'you guys'?" I asked.

"Dan, Sam, Eric—and probably you too, Riley," Bob said.

"Hey—I'm not part of this movie."

Dad put his arm around me. "Well, honey—you are now. You've been around all these people for a few months, and if anyone's done their homework, they probably figure that if you're around, so are Flip and Fawn."

I looked at Mom. "Can't you hunt these people down and arrest them?"

"I need time," she answered. "We don't really know who we're dealing with yet."

"Mom and I talked about this last night," Dad said. "It's summer, so we're going to take a little vacation, and while we're away, we'll try to get this mess figured out."

My head started spinning, and I knew it wasn't from hunger 'cause I had just stuffed myself.

"Wait. So you're saying we all have to hide out now? What about my friends?"

That's when I remembered ... "Yikes! Wait here. I have to check something."

I ran upstairs and looked at my phone. Still dead. I plugged it into the wall charger and turned it on. I watched the screen as it powered up, knowing exactly what I would see the minute everything connected...

Five texts from TJ:

Where R U???

We lost!!!!.

Rusty E'd.

In the loser bracket now.

Thanks for nuthin.

I was supposed to play in the softball tournament today! How could I forget that? This wasn't good. TJ would *never* forgive me. I threw myself on my bed and buried my face in my pillow.

But maybe if she knew what had happened...

I quickly grabbed my phone and wrote a text:

Accident on Half Dome

Flip almost died

Helicopter rescue

I'm in danger

Gotta hide out

There. She'd understand now.

But then I remembered Mom's words. *You can't tell anyone what happened today.*

So I deleted it all and wrote this instead:

Sorry TJ

Tired and sore

Then I hit send.

Dad called from downstairs.

"Riley! Can you come down? Someone's here to see you."

I had no clue who it could be. I half expected an angry TJ, swinging a bat.

It was Flip! I mean—Dan. This was all so confusing now! But it definitely couldn't be Flip, because his hair was combed and he had on a nice shirt with a collar and khaki pants. He was on crutches, and one foot had a dress shoe on it. The other had the cast.

"Who are you?" I joked, as I walked round and round him several times.

He held out his hand to shake mine.

"Daniel Stevens. But you can call me Flip. And I have some pretty awesome pictures to show you from yesterday." He held out a little piece of plastic. "The camera's trashed, but the memory card's still good. Wanna take a look?"

"Sure!" I ran to our computer in the living room, but Mom stopped me.

"First things first," she said. "You need to go upstairs and pack."

"For what?"

"Our vacation—did you forget already?" Dad handed me a suitcase. "Bring all your outdoor clothes. We're going to the Stevens' secret cabin."

Flip's eyes brightened. "I haven't been there for so long. You're gonna love it, Riley!"

"Where is it?' I asked.

Fawn walked in the room. "Can't tell you. Then it wouldn't be a secret."

Bob came in next. "It's all settled. I talked to Tyler—he'll be ready to fly everyone out in the jet tomorrow morning."

Flip pointed to me. "I'm not sure that gives this one enough time to pack. Have you seen her shoe collection?"

Then they were *all* looking at me. Flip (who's really Danny), Fawn (who's really Samantha), Eric (also known as the "Easter sneaker" or "Wiener dog"), Bob Hansen (who I guess was always Bob) and my mom and dad.

"So . . . I guess I'm not getting out of my contract, then?"

Mom crossed her arms. "Not a chance." Then she came and gave me a hug. "But we're all going to see this thing through together."

Chapter 52

Later that afternoon, my family came up with our "escape plan." My mom and dad had already taken Brady to grandma and grandpa's, so we decided he would stay there while Mom took a couple of days to get the police moving on the Flip and Fawn investigation. Dad and I would fly out with the Swiftriver gang in the morning, and then Mom and Brady would join us in a couple of days. Everything seemed smooth except one thing:

"*What* am I going to tell TJ?"

"The truth," Dad said. "Tell her we're going on a surprise vacation and you'll call her as soon as you can."

It sounded easy. But I couldn't do it. I knew TJ would ask tons of questions and I would probably end up saying too much. So I just turned off my phone.

Lying in bed that night, I stared at my ceiling and wished I could do the last few months over.

God, my life is so different now, and I'm not sure I like any of it.

If only I hadn't gone to Dad's office that day. If only I hadn't seen the shoes. If only I hadn't wanted to be a big shot. I could have played the whole season of softball, and I'd probably be staring at a four-foot-tall championship trophy right now. As I fell asleep, I prayed that this real nightmare would be over soon, and in the meantime, that I wouldn't have any more ridiculous dog dreams.

When I woke the next morning, I noticed that someone had put two more suitcases in my room. A note was hanging on one of them:

Make sure you pack all those Riley Mae shoes!

Ah, yes—the shoes. Those stupid things that got me into this whole mess. I pulled all of them out of the closet and threw them into the suitcases. Softball cleats, hikers, running shoes, cross-trainers ... shoes for anything that might come my way on this unexpected "vacation" at the "secret cabin."

"Great. No room for anything else." I plopped down on my bed and pounded my pillow a few times while I tried to figure out where I would pack the rest of my stuff.

Hurry up, Riley. You don't have time for a temper tantrum. You're on the run, remember?

I grabbed my backpack. Maybe I could shove some clothes in there if I emptied the books out. One of the books I pulled out was my Bible.

I opened it up to where the little tinfoil bookmark

said "Ephesians 6," the part about putting on the armor of God. I grinned a little as I thought of my crazy brother wearing all the pieces of armor that we made in children's church. My eyes stuck on verse 15:

"For shoes, put on the peace that comes from the Good News so you will be fully prepared."

I put the Bible on the nightstand and took a deep breath. Okay, I could do this.

You're always tougher than you think.

I quickly threw on some jeans and a t-shirt and put my hair up in a ponytail. I grabbed a couple big tote bags from the closet and started shoving stuff in: phone; phone charger; favorite clothes; secret chocolate stash; toothbrush; softball glove; picture of me, TJ, and Rusty eating brownies; and a little stuffed Panda bear that Brady gave me for my birthday.

Dad came up to help me take some of my bags. "Do you have everything you need?"

I scanned my room. How was I supposed to know what I would need for this crazy trip? "Yeah, I think I got it all."

"Good. Well then, let's go." He clunk, clunk, clunked my suitcase all the way down the stairs. He hollered back up. "I can see you didn't forget the Riley Mae shoes!"

I looked back at my bedroom one more time. When would I next sleep here? I grabbed my pillow and tucked it under my arm. The pink blanket I got at the hospital peeked out at me from under my bedspread, and I threw that around my neck.

That's when I spotted my Bible on my nightstand.

"Whoa! Can't forget the Good News shoes."

Mom yelled from downstairs. "Riley, please tell me you're ready."

I tucked the Bible under my other arm and grinned.

Whatever happens next, I'll be ready.

Acknowledgements

Writing this series has been one of the great joys of my life. But I couldn't do it alone! Many thanks go to …

My Savior and Lord, Jesus Christ—For loving me enough to die for me. And then loving me enough to live in me! Apart from You, I can do nothing.

My steadfast husband Mike—For being my best friend for the last thirty-four years, and for always believing that I am better than I really am. I love you!

My encouraging family—For your support and prayers and for always assuming I'd publish a book someday. Mom—here it is! I know you've been waiting a long time.

Monika Jagger—For supplying iced tea (with good ice), brownies, peanut M&Ms and lots of laughter during hundreds of writing sessions.

Judy Gordon Morrow—For being such a loving mentor and prayer partner. You taught me by example how to walk hand in hand with Jesus. Blessing upon blessing to you, my dear friend!

Bill Myers—For being the "real deal," and for teaching me the essentials of writing for today's kids. Also, for brainstorming with me at the coffee shop at Mt. Hermon, and for encouraging me to actually talk to some editors about my work.

Kim Childress—For your encouragement and prayers. The dedication and hard work by you and your entire team has made this experience a joy and a blessing for me. Just keep swimming, because kids need to keep reading!

And … To all the kids at Golden Hills Community Church in Paso Robles, CA, and Northside Christian Church in Clovis, CA.

(And really to all the kids out there):
> You are the reason I write.
> You are beautiful. You are talented.
> You are God's masterpiece!

And you have a mission:
> Share the Good News of Jesus with a lost world.
> I know you can do it.
> I'll be praying for you.
> Write me and let me know how I can help!

Love, Jill

We want to hear from you. Please send your comments about this book to us in care of zreview@zondervan.com. Thank you.

 ZONDER**kidz**